VAST

Book Three of The Scorpion Chronicles

Russell Turnbull

Russell Turnbull Studios

Russell Turnbull Studios
Carlisle, Pennsylvania

Second Edition
Trade Paperback ISBN: 979-8989088522

Cover designed by Miblart.

THE SCORPION CHRONICLES

Hollow: Book One

Dark: Book Two

Vast: Book Three

THANKS

I would like to thank and/or mention the following:

My wife, Tania

Michele Golden

Mr. Stephen King

Mr. R.A. Salvatore

The Pittsburgh Pirates

The Boston Red Sox

The Omni Hotel

Miblart Cover Design

Keri at New Shelves Books &

My Chocolate Shoppe, Charlottesville, VA

DEDICATION

For Tabitha Charlotte

CONTENTS

Author's Notes

Welcome back to the Realm of Beornan Heafod in this, the third installment to The Scorpion Chronicles.

This was originally intended to be the finale to a trilogy, but I've fallen in love with these characters and have come up with even more interesting characters that I'm sure you'll fall in love with as well.

As with the preceding installments, you will undoubtedly find foreign words that you cannot translate easily. They are either archaic words not used in today's languages, or (most likely) Latin. I have also mixed a bit of Irish, Gaelic and French (among other) words and terms within, because they fit their given situations and explain things a bit better than common English words and terms could. If you find this confusing, I apologize in advance. (You can use Google Translate to decipher almost everything within this saga.)

I would like to thank those who stood behind me throughout the writing of this saga: your patience and support means the world to me.

The wedding sequence is written (almost) word for word from my (and Tania's) wedding ceremony.

Thanks...

Russell Turnbull

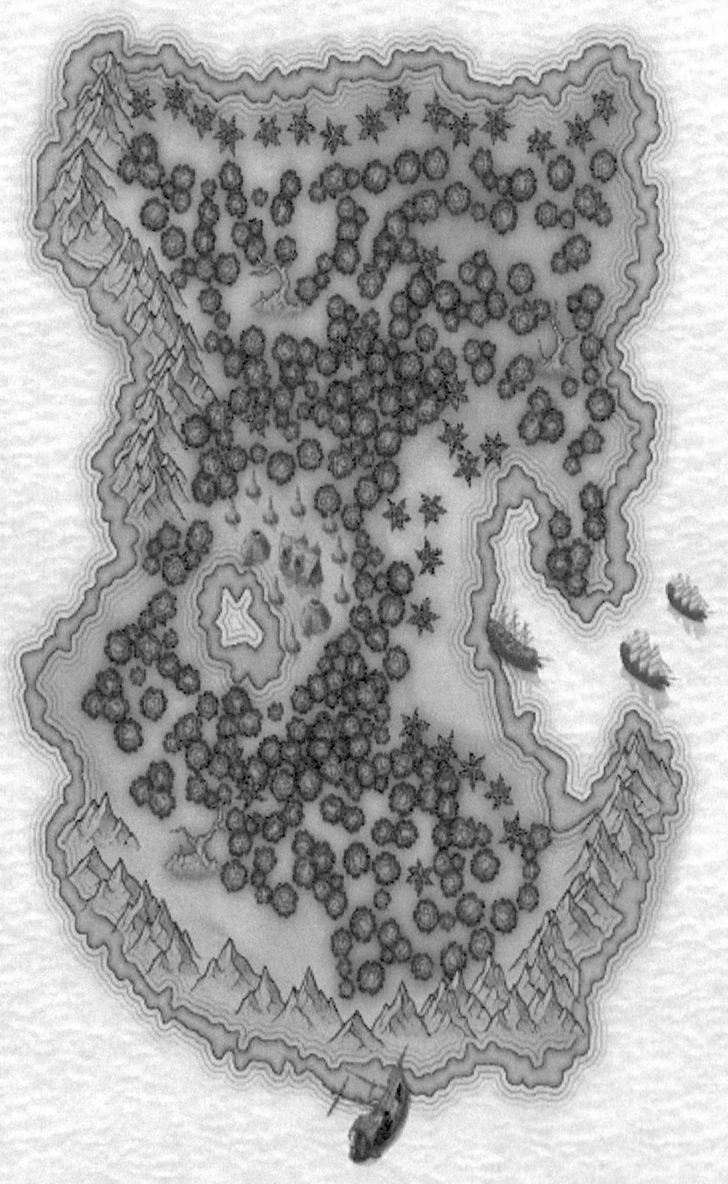

ERRFORDLAND

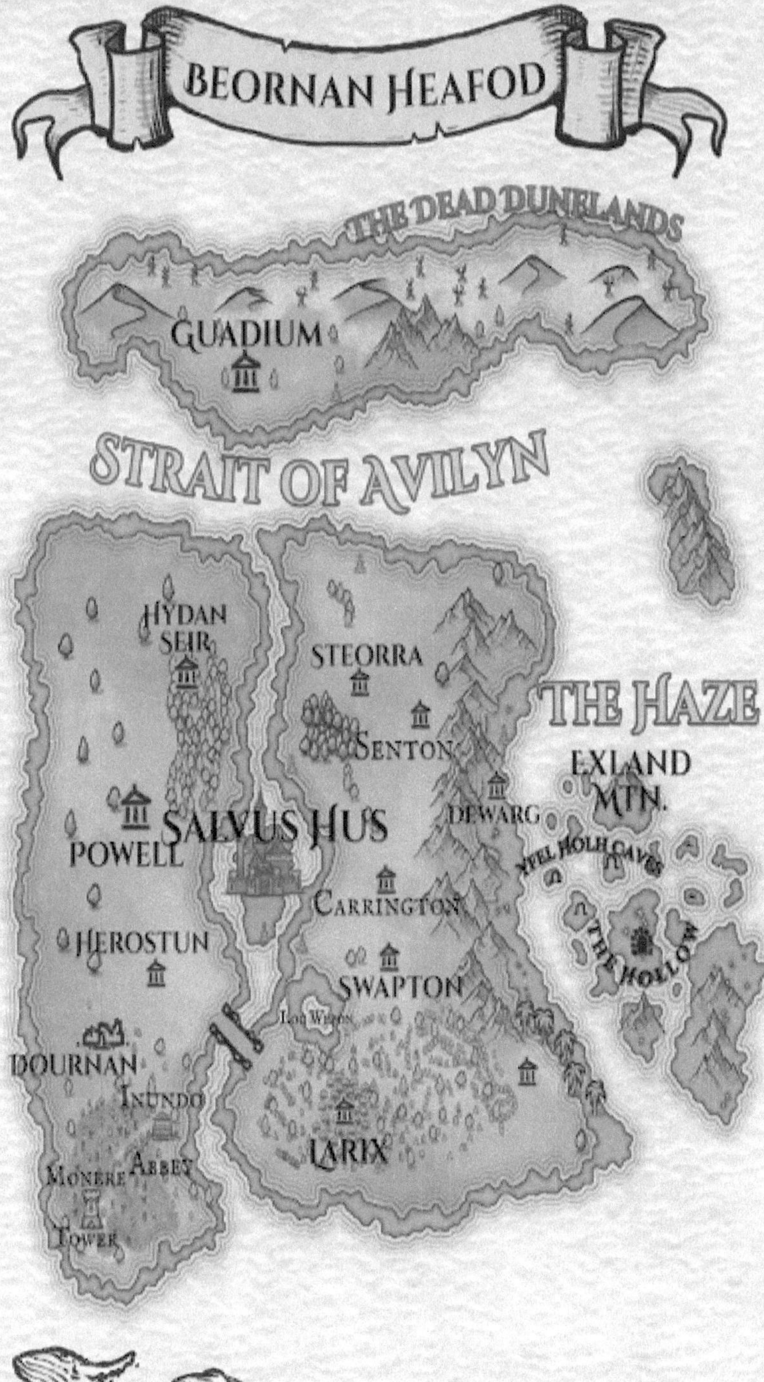

BEORNAN HEAFOD
THE DEAD DUNELANDS
GUADIUM
STRAIT OF AVILYN
HYDAN SEIR
STEORRA
THE HAZE
EXLAND MTN.
SENTON
SALVUS HUS
DEWARG
POWELL
NYEL HOLH CAVES
HEROSTUN
CARRINGTON
THE HOLLOW
SWAPTON
Lon Wuon
DOURNAN
INUNDO
LARIX
MONERE ABBEY
TOWER

PROLOGUE

L and was nowhere in sight, and it was raining so hard that we could barely see each other when we appeared back on the deck of The Scorpion.

"Where are we?" I asked, having to yell loudly over the sound of the torrential storm beating on the ship.

"I have no idea!" Byron yelled back, "I'm not a sailor; I'm a land loving soldier!"

"We have to find Captain Waxx!" I hollered back.

"Below decks!" Loher called and grabbed my hand.

We ran through the rain, barely able to see where we were going, but well enough to notice that there was no one else in sight.

"Where is the crew?" I asked whoever could hear me.

"What?" Byron called from behind.

"I said," I slowed and let him catch up, "where is the crew? There's no one on deck!"

"That's what I thought you said!" Byron yelled over the rain.

"Come on!" Loher yelled, "Let's get below!"

My stomach hurt, not only from eating too much of Shannon's pasketty, but now from the gripping thought that we had been 'blinked' to a derelict ship drifting far off into nowhere.

This **was** The Scorpion, no other ship that I've seen looked like a giant floating golden statue of a scorpion; she was one-of-a-kind.

As we ran to the steps that led to the ship's belly, we could see a light coming from down below.

I tugged Loher's arm and made her stop.

I leaned up close to her ear and said, "Let me go first, there might be trouble!"

Loher agreed and motioned Byron to stand by.

The veteran soldier complied.

I remembered that I had procured a cloak of shadows from the tower, so I slipped the hood over my head and vanished.

Invisible, I slowly slipped my way carefully down the steps and peeked around the corner into the hold.

Everyone was down there, the captain, the entire crew and our companions, accompanied by a large group of orc marauders and a single, elderly human male.

The human was dressed in purple robes of the magic sort, and I assumed that he was in control of the orc marauders.

Balt looked beat up quite badly, but Brother Fost was tending to his wounds.

Meeka was bound with ties and gagged, while Kuchoff was lying on the floor, not moving; I couldn't tell if he was alive or dead.

They must have taken the crew by surprise, because I didn't see any dead orcs anywhere; the storm must have been their cover.

Then, the thought occurred to me; perhaps this was an unnatural storm, created by the robe clad human...?

I snuck back up the steps.

"We need that new bow of yours," I whispered in Loher's ear while holding a hand up to Byron, letting him know to be patient.

The three of us huddled together as I explained the situation in detail, and we came up with a plan.

Loher strung up her new bow as Byron and I readied our blades.

On the silent count of three, Loher cloaked herself and then led the way down the steps and fired multiple arrows at the purple robed human, taking the whole party, our companions included, by complete surprise.

As Loher's arrows found purchase in the body of the robed one, our blades found their marks as well, as one by one, the orcs fell.

Balt took this chance to grab a fallen sword and join in the fight until he could get his ruddy little hands on his beloved Great Axe.

Brother Fost rushed over and cut Meeka free and then attended to the apparently still living Kuchoff.

The sounds of angry battle raged on below decks as sailors took up arms and grievously joined the cause.

We made quick work of the enemy as they were outnumbered almost three to one.

"Dem sharks be eatin' good tonight, Bruddah!" Captain Waxx cheered as we met among the corpses of the fallen.

After a moment's pause to catch our breath and survey the damage, my curiosity got the best of me, "What happened, Captain?" I asked.

"De storm juss came outta nowhere, Mon," the captain began, "an' dey juss appeared outta nowhere too, juss like you and yor friends do."

"No ship?" I asked.

The captain's eyes went wide when he finally took a good look at me, and then a big smile sprang out upon his lips, "Yor not a vampire no-more!" He realized.

The storm had slowed down to a steady rain and continued to weaken to an eventual stop as the wind had all but died away.

The glorious sun began to peek out from behind the clouds, burning them away and delivering a nice, clear, calm day.

"No ship?" I repeated and returned a finally fangless smile.

"No, Mon," the captain answered, "no ship, juss a big lightning crack an' a puff of brown smoke an' den dare dey were."

"Obvious magic of some sort," I concluded.

"Perhaps yor lady wizard friend can tell us what it was, Bruddah," Captain Waxx chuckled, relieved that there was no lasting damage to his ship or crew.

We ventured up the steps and surveyed the surrounding area to see where we were.

The decks were rain soaked, but the crewmen were well on their way drying it up the best that they could.

"Do you know where we are?" I asked the captain as he checked with his telescope and sextant.

"No," he answered, his lips now vacant of a trace of a smile, "not a clue, Mon."

My now beating heart sank a bit.

The captain nodded and hurriedly walked away to talk to a few of his trusted crewmen about rectifying the situation.

I stood there for a moment or two to collect my thoughts and stare out to sea in hopes that I would see land at best, or perhaps another ship.

My companions were searching the bodies of the dead orc marauders or helping The Scorpion's crew clean up the mess.

The corpses were searched, stripped of anything useful and then tossed, one by one overboard.

I began to stroll about the ship and survey the situation and as I did, I passed by members of the crew that looked pleased and relieved as they saw me, that I was no longer undead.

I decided to seek out my companions.

The first of my companions that I found were Byron, Brother Fost and Kuchoff.

"How is he?" I asked after coaxing the priest away from Kuchoff.

"He'll live," the halfling answered, "he is a very brave young man. As soon as one of the orcs grabbed Meeka, he attacked. Unfortunately, he did minor damage to her assailant and was thrashed within a thread of his life and left for dead." The priest looked at me, "Another question is, how are you doing now that you're 'alive' again?" He asked with a relieved smile and concern in his eyes.

"I'll live," I answered with a wink and smile at my echoed reply and motioned him back to his patient, "I'll check on you in a bit."

"We will be here," Fost said and turned back to Kuchoff, "he's not going anywhere for a while."

I walked away, not knowing what to do or how to feel now; I decided to catch up with Balt.

I found him and Loher searching the remainder of the orc corpses before some crew members took them away to be shark food.

Meeka was leaning over the dead human, reading a small book she had found in his robes; she wouldn't let anyone near him until she was sure she had everything the corpse had to offer.

Loher's arrows still protruded from his chest along with one expertly placed arrow directly in the center of his forehead.

I walked over and tried to yank the arrow from his forehead.

It took some effort and some wiggling, but I got it out with no damage to the arrowhead.

Blood and grey brain matter dripped from the sharpened tip and made a slight splattering sound when it contacted the floor.

I inspected the projectile and was amazed at the nearly perfect condition it was still in.

"Here, Loher," I said as I offered the arrow back to her, "A souvenir."

She took the arrow, looked at it, shrugged her shoulders, smiled and put the arrow back into her quiver, "Thanks," she said and returned to the corpse she was searching.

"Oi, Mate!" Balt exclaimed.

I turned and looked at the dwarf.

"Ye be alive!" He testified.

I just smiled as the dwarf stood and looked at me.

"Bout time," he grunted and went back to the sword he was inspecting.

"Meeka," I softly called to get her attention, but not to disturb her too much as she was probably deeply consumed in whatever magic book she was reading.

After a short pause, the wizard looked up and lightly shook the cobwebs out of her mind, returning to our version of reality.

She smiled as she realized that I was no longer a vampire, "How is Kuchoff?"

"Brother Fost says that he'll live and be good as new in no time," I half lied.

"That orc trounced him pretty badly and there was nothing anyone could do to stop it," she reported and looked back down at the cover of the book she held.

"Do you have any idea who that man was?" I asked, trying not to sound too interested.

She looked down at the corpse in front of her and frowned, "No," she shook her head, "but these robes look familiar, I'm sure I have seen them before. I think they belong to some sort of religious order or cult or something, but who, I couldn't begin to say."

Her answer shocked me and made chills slowly run up my spine.

"So, this wasn't some sort of random attack," I rhetorically commented.

"No," she agreed, "This had purpose behind it, but who was he and what did he want?"

"I believe the proper term to use would be 'they' not 'he,' Meeka," I added, "if he belonged to some sort of order, or sect, or cult or something, he did not act alone. I think we may not have seen the last of them."

"Like I said before," she reminded, "I can't be sure of where or what he came from." The wizard lowered her eyes and opened the book again, to the page she was studying, and continued to read.

I watched my companions delve into their chosen duties for a while and then decided to return to the bridge to see if the captain had any luck finding out where we were.

When I surfaced back to the deck, I saw that the crew had everything back in proper order as if the skirmish had never taken place; all but the crew members that were still hauling orc corpses to the railing and dumping them overboard.

Curiously, I looked behind the ship and saw a trail of bodies in our wake; I shuddered and forced a chuckle.

When I arrived at the bridge, Captain Waxx and his helmsman had very confused looks on their faces while leaning over a map spread out across the table.

"Any luck finding out where we are?" I innocently asked.

The captain and helmsman looked up and Captain Waxx shook his head, "Not a clue, Mon, I 'ave been ev'ry where on dees wat'rs an' know my way to ev'ry port, but we cannot find our bearings no matter 'ow much we be lookin'."

"So, we're lost," I muttered.

"Correct, Mon, an' it gets worse," he warned and pointed to the horizon.

I looked out, over the sea and all I saw were dark clouds surrounding us as if we were in the eye of a great storm, only this storm was closing in on us.

That pain in my stomach went from a dull throb from too much food to a sharp stab of anxiety, fear and worry in an instant.

The captain and helmsman went back to looking at the map and my thoughts went to my companions below deck.

I had to warn them.

"How long?" I asked.

"We be battenin' down de hatches in less dan an hour, Mon," the captain half groaned, "Dis is gonna be a bad one."

CHAPTER ONE

THE LULL BEFORE THE STORM

I excused myself from the ship's bridge and rushed as fast as I could to the hold to find and warn my companions of the impending doom approaching.

They were all still busy with their chosen duties as I noisily blundered down the steps; their heads sprang up in excited curiosity as I all but tumbled into the room.

It was instantly more than obvious to them that I was the bearer of bad news.

"What is it, McLaaud?" Loher asked with no hesitation.

Slightly out of breath, I coughed, "We are drifting within the eye of probably the worst storm the captain has ever encountered," I looked from face to face to gauge my companions' reactions, so far, all were remaining almost as calm as just before, "The crew is beginning to 'batten down the hatches', whatever that means, but I'm sure we are all about to have the ride of our lives, very soon."

"It means," Brother Fost offered, "they are securing the loose parts of the ship and making it as watertight as they can because we are about to get extremely wet, all at once, for a very long time."

"Tat be a bad ting, Mate," Balt added with a slight chuckle.

"This is no time for jokes, Balt," Meeka scolded.

"Take ease, Lass," the dwarf sighed, "we doon't wanna frighten ta boy-o, now, do we?"

The wizard frowned at the warrior and then turned back to attend to the injured boy.

"Is there anything we can do to help?" Byron offered,

"I'm sure the crew could use a hand out there," I suggested, "although without knowing what you're doing, you might just be in their way."

"The best course of action for you land lovers," a sailor obnoxiously began after overhearing our conversation while he and a few others were retrieving planking from the hold, "is to stay put down here and take care of your wounded; it would be safer for us all."

"I guess that settles it," Loher announced, "we'll secure what we can down here and stay out of their way unless asked to assist."

"I'm not certain how long or how bad this is going to be," I added, "but it looks like it's going to become horribly dangerous out there."

Balt grumbled something about redundancy as he returned his attention to the task at hand.

In the temporary calm still, we could hear the rushing footsteps of the crew above us, along with the pounding of nails and slamming of planks against the windows of the ship as the crew reinforced The Scorpion's structural integrity.

Orders were being called out in semi-frantic tones as the wind suddenly began to intensify.

Moments later, fat raindrops the size of lemons began to crash down on the decks, quickly turning into hailstones of equal or greater size.

The damage from their impact was devastating.

Crewmen were being rushed down to the hold, suffering from trauma to the head, shoulders and neck, most bleeding profusely from open wounds.

Sadly, a few were set in the far corner of the hold and covered with strips of old torn up sails; they were dead.

"We have got to do something!" Meeka shrieked.

Brother Fost was already rushing about from crewman to crewman, healing who he could and making comfortable those which he couldn't.

The rest of us followed suit, creating an improvised triage, and began comforting the injured and covering the dead.

Incredibly and very suddenly...Silence.

The weather had stopped.

No sound.

The Scorpion began to settle.

We all looked around in astonishment.

"Somting un-natural be happenin' e're," Captain Waxx stammered.

A gasp escaped from Meeka's lips, and she began to point towards Kuchoff.

The kid was wide awake and holding his hands out above his head, pantomiming a shielding action with his hands.

A bright blue-green glow was emanating through the cracks in the deck boards and from beyond the cargo hold door.

Byron cautiously investigated the door, cracking it open slightly and peering outside.

"If I wasn't seeing this with my own two eyes, I would never believe it," He smiled as he swung the door wide open.

We could all see the storm still raging on outside, but there was a bright blue-green energy dome surrounding The Scorpion, deflecting the hailstones, wind and rain, keeping us safe.

"He's still weak," Brother Fost warned in a worried tone, "how long can you hold this, Kuchoff?"

Unwavering and unblinking, Kuchoff didn't answer.

Without a word, Captain Waxx and a few others scrambled up the steps and began to survey the area.

—◆—

"Land Ho!" A voice suddenly bellowed.

It was the one phrase we were all eager to hear.

"Can we make it?" I called as I too, bolted up into the open.

"Not wit'out no wind," the captain replied.

"Tell your men to set the sails in that direction," I suggested sternly.

"Den de kid will retract de bubble?" Waxx half asked, half protested.

"It may be the only way," I answered.

He stood there and stared at me as he quickly weighed out the options in his head and then, once his decision was made, he called out the order and the crew jumped to it, "Attention on Deck," the captain announced, "Pr'pare for a crash beaching!"

Sails were set to receive the impending massive amounts of squall-like winds in order to direct The Scorpion toward the land mass.

As soon as all of the crewmen were finished and safely below, Meeka assured Kuchoff that it was beneficial to stop his Psi-dome.

The boy finally blinked his eyes and produced a faint smile as he relaxed and allowed the wind to slam into the ship's sales like a giant fist.

We felt the ship lurch into motion and travel in speeds comparable to when we outran the water elemental in the Strait of Avilyn a year ago, however, this time, Captain Waxx, or anyone else for that matter, was not smiling.

Chunks of ice and freezing rain pelted down on the ship, punching several large, gaping holes into the deck.

The sound was deafening.

After what seemed like only a minute or two, The Scorpion beached violently on the shore of the mid-sized island that the look-out had spotted.

The sounds of splintering wood and scraping rock echoed above the relentless downpour of the torrential wind and rain.

"At least the hail has stopped," Loher uttered, breaking the wordless silence as everyone gathered themselves after the crash.

Water continued to pour into the hold from the breaches caused in the crash while the wind and rain outside continued to rage on, battering the top and sides of the now unmovable ship.

Many of the crewmen began to gather supplies while a second group assembled an away team to explore the island we had become beached upon.

⸰⸰⸰

"If you don't mind, Captain," I offered, "a few of my men and I would like to accompany your team on the away mission."

The captain silently nodded his agreement, or perhaps it was only an acknowledgment, his back was turned to me and his head was hanging a bit lower than I cared to observe.

He was obviously concerned and upset about the state of his beloved ship, as any captain would rightfully be.

"Will ye be joinin' us Cap'n?" Balt inquired.

"Aye, Mon," the captain slowly and quietly answered.

This pleased the dwarven warrior enough that he was compelled to jovially slug Captain Waxx on the shoulder; the impact must have rattled something inside of the captain, bringing him slightly out of his gloom and made him smile a bit.

It has been said, time and time again, that there is always safety in numbers, but in my recent experience, that is not always true.

Experience is key.

If the team members of an away mission are inexperienced or weak, the more people on the team, the better and safer that team would, presumably be, but in our present situation, we had several veteran fighters and explorers, so a smaller team would suffice.

After what seemed like hours of discussion and careful planning, we decided on a group of five consisting of me and Balt, along with Captain Waxx and two of his crew; large men with large, bladed swords, the likes I've only seen in drawings about the now extinct cyclops race.

The cyclops once lived on the most northern isle in the realm.

It was once a green and flourishing area, generally peaceful for thousands of years or more.

Occasional battles for territorial rights with the hill giants would erupt, but would quickly and peacefully resolve... until the hill giants suddenly became increasingly greedier and violently tried to wage a full-scale war to take over the cyclops' homeland.

Naturally, the cyclops revolted with force and 'The Great Battle' had begun.

With so many warriors of each respective species, there were plenty on each side to keep the war violently heated for centuries...

...until the dragons took over...

The rest is ancient history.

I digress.

You've heard this all before.

The swords carried by these two sailors must have been wielded by cyclops warriors during that war, confirming truth in legend for me, once again.

Before the away team embarked on our mission, I called a semi-private meeting of my immediate companions.

"While we are out, exploring this island," I suggested, "see what you can do to help the crew, but stay out of their way if you find yourself in it."

"We had already planned that," Brother Fost assured, "although, and I'm sure you'll agree, my first priority is to Kuchoff's well-being and then to the injured sailors."

Loher put her hand on my shoulder and looked me in the eye, "Don't worry about us," she added with a slight smile and a wink, "I'll keep everyone in line."

"I'm sure ye will, Lass," Balt quietly chuckled.

Loher thumbed a note from her bow string in reply and grinned.

As an afterthought, I leaned in and whispered to Byron, "Set up a separate, yet adjoining camp for the seven of us. I'm not sure that some of the crew is completely satisfied with my transformation back from being one of the undead."

Byron clasped my hand and gripped it tightly, "Consider it done, my friend."

"Be casual about it," I added.

Byron smiled and nodded.

The storm had finally weakened substantially to light yet steady rain.

Captain Waxx and his two men were already prepared to go, so Balt and I gathered our gear and deployed into the unknown along with them.

Chapter Two

INCERTUM

The sky was beginning to look less and less angry as the day ebbed on and it looked as though we would have quite a pleasant evening, assuming we didn't run into any hostile natives.

After a moment, the rain had completely stopped, and the sun began to peek out from behind its shield of clouds.

The shore of the island consisted of rocks with stretches of sand and ground up shell, or some similar material.

"Too bad we didn't run de ship into one o' dees sandy stretches," Captain Waxx rhetorically commented.

We continued walking.

Working our way from the beach inward, we began to enter a typical forest, consisting of oaks, maples, pines, ash, birch and other similar type trees.

The further we traveled into the trees, the denser they became, as well as the grasses, ferns, vines, and other undergrowth.

The two sailors in the lead began to use their swords to help blaze a trail for easier navigation.

Suddenly, an odd realization occurred to me...

'Why is the ground not saturated by all of the rain from the storm?'
I thought to myself.

I leaned down and picked up a bit of soil from beside my boot.

It was entirely dry to the touch and quite crumbly under a small
amount of pressure.

Captain Waxx noticed my movements, "What be it, Mon?" He
asked.

"With as much rain as we had just gotten," I began, "shouldn't the
ground be saturated and muddy?"

The captain shuffled his foot in the dirt and kicked up a small puff
of dust, "Yor right!" He breathed, "Dat be a bit strange, Mon."

"Maybe t'is part o' ta island got missed by ta rain?" Balt offered.

We looked up into the canopy of trees and were surprised to see
little to no sunlight filtering through, yet the ambient lighting around
us was bright enough for us to easily see, as if we were standing on the
beach in early evening.

"I guess that explains it," I rhetorically thought out loud, "sort of."

Captain Waxx and the others must have accepted that explanation,
for they simply shrugged off the oddness and continued to move along
the path the sailors were creating.

Besides, dwarves don't generally believe in magic, although I think
Balt may be coming around to it.

As we moved along, I couldn't help but to reflect on the odd
lighting within the trees; it was bothering me that I couldn't figure it
out.

I was born and raised within an enchanted forest and have witnessed some strange and mystical occurrences, but until then, I had
never seen anything like the odd lighting, as subtle as it was.

Reflecting on my memories of my own homeland of the Seolfer
Wudu, some of the strangeness here in these woods seemed common-

place to me, yet I couldn't understand why my companions didn't seem affected by it until I pointed it out.

Perhaps they were expecting differences and were accepting of it?

But why would they be **expecting** differences?

I decided to keep any other strangeness to myself, unless I felt that we may be endangered in any way.

Aside from the lack of moisture in the ground and the strange ambient lighting, these woods seemed fairly normal.

There were birds singing, small woodland creatures such as chipmunks, rabbits and odd-looking squirrels scampering about, normal foliage growing and even small spiders, extremely large butterflies and other various insects; yet I still couldn't shake the feeling that there was something else that was very strange about this forest.

I just couldn't put my finger on it.

"Somethin' ahead of us, Captain," one of the hulking sailors announced in a hushed voice.

The captain put his hand up in the air, about shoulder level, and the group stopped.

I slipped up front to see what it was.

When I reached point position, I noticed that the lighting had become brighter up ahead.

I looked up to the canopy and saw that there was a moderate sized clearing ahead; we were still standing safely within the tree line.

I slowly began to crouch down and waved my hand in a palm down motion, silently suggesting to the rest to do the same.

The team complied.

The captain cautiously made his way to my side, "What do you see, Mon?"

I pointed to the clearing in the canopy and then slowly, with a slight circling motion, lowered my hand to the area a short distance in front of us.

The captain nodded, understanding that I was telling him about the clearing.

I looked at Balt to see that he was looking at me as well, smiling and gripping his Great Axe; he would tighten his grip on the handle and then loosen it up, alternating this motion as a way of asking me if there was a battle to be won.

I raised a single index finger at him, telling him to be patient and that I didn't know yet.

I've learned to appreciate his willingness, almost eagerness, to engage an enemy, if need be, but I never completely understood Balt's eagerness to commence battle at any given time.

Perhaps he had either a blood lust or a death wish.

Death wish can be ruled out, because he always fought so hard to win every battle and if by some rare chance he were to be wounded, he would fight even harder to stay alive, just to continue to fight.

A man with a death wish would just allow defeat and die right away.

I'm almost certain it was a bloodlust...or insanity.

(I ramble.)

The captain's two sailors were crouched down as well, but neither of them looked very eager to fight, although ready to, with weapons in hand.

I motioned the group to stay put and then slowly crept closer to the tree line at the edge of the clearing.

The clearing spread out into an oblong meadow large enough to fit a small town, complete with what looked, from my position, to be a small lagoon or natural pool.

Lush, knee-high grasses carpeted the virtually flat area, large colorful birds were beginning to roost on low hanging branches and a sweet fragrant breeze lightly blew through; it looked almost like a created paradise.

(Created by whom?)

This was too good to be true; I didn't trust it and it was beginning to get dark, so I crept back to the team and explained the situation and suggested that we go back to The Scorpion.

We needed to check on and inform the rest of our companions.

The captain agreed and we went back to the beach.

⚬

As we arrived on the beach, I noticed that the supplies that were saved from the wreckage of The Scorpion were organized nicely, and a camp had been set.

Brother Fost and a few sailors had caught and cleaned a mess of fish that the Priest was cooking up, Kuchoff was up and slowly walking around with Meeka's guidance while Loher, Byron and a few of the sailors were patrolling the perimeter of the camp; we were met by one of the sailors on our way in.

The rest of the sailors were still busy working on repairing the damage to The Scorpion's hull, but the light was dimming fast, and efforts were slowly winding down.

The sky looked clear, and stars began to twinkle in unfamiliar patterns, assuring us once again that we were completely lost.

My team, along with the captain and his senior staff gathered around the fire and discussed our predicament and possible options.

The captain informed us that he and his crew had no idea how long they would need to complete the repairs to The Scorpion and get us under way.

They didn't have the supplies to complete the repairs, so they would have to cut down a bunch of trees and mill some lumber to fashion some boards strong enough to fix the hull breaches.

"As long as we don't run into any hostile natives," I reflected, "I'm quite satisfied with spending some time here."

"Aye," Balt agreed, "but a few hostiles would be welcomed."

"That clearing you mentioned seems like a good place to possibly set up a more permanent camp in the meantime," Loher suggested, "and we may be safer there."

"We still 'ave ta explore and secure ta area first, Lass," Balt enlightened without thinking.

Loher just shot him a look of distaste as she tossed a twig into the fire and then searched the immediate surroundings with her eyes for another.

Balt was obviously excited about exploring the new area in hopes that we would, in fact, encounter an enemy of some sort.

"I'm confident that Kuchoff will be well enough tomorrow," Meeka stated, "so we can go with you. I'm sure one of us would be able to detect any magical goings on in that clearing you described... if there is anything to be detected, that is."

"I'll go along as well," Brother Fost announced, "In case the kid has a relapse, and besides, perhaps I will find some good cooking and healing herbs along the way.

"You're not leaving me behind," Byron added with a smile, "I still have a good sword arm and I'm always up for an adventure.

"I guess the whole team is going," I laughed and put my hands up in a surrendering motion.

The sun had completely set, and the night sang out with the music that only the nocturnal creatures of the forest knew how to play.

The music was accompanied by the soothing sounds of the ocean waves breaking on the rocks nearby.

It was relaxing and soon, all except for the posted guards, were fast asleep.

Loher woke me from a peaceful slumber; it was still dark. "It's our turn, McLaaud."

"Our turn for what?" I asked, still more than half asleep.

"To keep watch," she giggled and nudged me a bit harder with her boot.

I got up and grabbed my gear.

The night music was still in full orchestral swing, telling me that all was right around us.

I sniffed the night air and smelled nothing odd, so I stoked the fire and looked around.

My eyesight was comparable to how it was when undead, which made me feel a bit anxious.

The firelight grew into a soft warm glow, allowing me to observe the sleeping group of people I had grown to love and trust.

(The family I never had.)

Kuchoff and Meeka were snuggled up to each other; adoptive mother and son, Byron, although not sleeping, was laying close by, staring off into the stars, a calm look upon his face.

Brother Fost was fast asleep, lying curled up in a tight ball in the tall grass, lightly snoring.

My eyes then focused on Loher, the firelight casting a ghostly glow around her, revealing the most beautiful of features I have ever seen in a woman, elf, human or otherwise; I found her absolutely irresistible, and I counted myself lucky to have her by my side.

I decided that when we make it back to the Seolfer Wudu, I would ask her to marry me... perhaps sooner.

My thoughts and adoring gaze were suddenly ripped away by the sound of a snapping twig close behind me.

I grabbed the hilt of my sword and spun around, about to draw my blade when I noticed it was Balt, carelessly walking up behind me.

"Wot?" The dwarf asked, confused with the sight of my hand on my sword, "I hadda wee."

I relaxed a bit and noticed that the night music had quieted a bit, but was slowly regaining its former glory, which made me relax a bit more.

"Be more careful with your steps in the future," I half hissed at his carelessness.

He bowed an apology, realizing his folly and shot me a grin.

I playfully punched him in the arm as a way of letting him know he was forgiven, and we strolled up to Loher.

Loher was staring out to sea with an odd look on her face.

"You miss home?" I asked.

"No," she answered, "not really," she answered.

"What then?" I pried.

"I just don't like being stuck where I don't know where I am," she admitted.

"T'at makes two o' us," Balt agreed.

We stood in silence for a while, staring blankly into the darkness over the sea, until I remembered that we should walk the perimeter of the camp.

It was our turn to keep watch anyway.

I circled to the left while Balt circled to the right and Loher cut through the middle.

We all ended up meeting somewhere in the center of the other side, so Balt and I passed each other and continued on the other's reverse path as Loher turned around and reversed her own path as well.

We continued this action irregularly for the next three hours until the sun began to rise from what looked like the middle of the sea.

A beautiful sunrise, it started off slowly at first and then gained a bit more speed the further it rose.

Sailors began to wake and take over, letting the three of us get a bit of rest before the day officially began.

Loher and I decided to sit by the dying fire, while Balt was almost instantly asleep and snoring loudly, leaning against a tree.

By the time my whole team, sans Balt, was awake, the repair crew had eaten, exercised like they did every morning and began to work on The Scorpion.

Captain Waxx finally emerged from within the ship, probably woken by the sounds of repair, and gathered a small crew to accompany us in exploration; the two big sailors from the day before included.

"Yor whole team be going, Mon?" He asked, a bit cheerier than the previous day.

"That's right," I answered.

"Less dat I be having to bring along den," he smiled and dismissed over half of the men he had chosen; they immediately returned to repairing the ship.

"Will they be okay without any of us around?" Meeka asked.

"We be pirates, Ma'am," Captain Waxx chuckled, "Dey be okay."

Meeka blushed and looked after Kuchoff as an escape from further embarrassment.

Brother Fost arrived at the huddle carrying a large bag, apparently stuffed with food, water and other needed supplies.

Byron took up the bag and put it in his backpack.

"I notice," Captain Waxx observed, "yor team work well toget'er, Mon."

"We should," I agreed, "we've been together long enough."

"Some longer than others," Byron added.

"Years for some of us," Kuchoff added and smiled at Meeka.

The captain cocked his head to the side in wonder, "What happened to de knight you had in yor group, Mon?"

"Dead." Balt spat bluntly as he stopped snoring and opened his eyes.

"Balt!" Meeka hissed.

"Wot?" Balt asked, confused, rubbing the sleep dust from his eyes.

"We met up with an enormous spider that overpowered the team, so he sacrificed himself to save the rest of us," I explained.

"A noble gesture," Captain Waxx commented, "We shall celebrate his life, Mon."

"Was he... eaten?" A sailor nervously gulped.

"Na," Balt responded and pointed at Meeka, "she blowed 'im up along wit ta spider b'fore it ever got a chance."

Meeka's face drained of all color and went ashen white.

"Balt!" Loher hissed.

"Wot?" The dwarven warrior innocently wondered aloud.

<hr>

It was the beginning of a gorgeous day; the weather was kind, not a cloud in the sky.

The night music had stopped hours ago. It had slowly changed to a quieter, but no less apparent symphony of bird songs and parrot caws.

The path we had blazed the day before was easy to follow, especially with that strange ambient lighting within the thick forest.

So odd.

Meeka and Kuchoff both agreed that it was strange, but neither of them could determine whether it was magical in nature or not; the question still plagues me to this day.

Brother Fost was having an exceptional time, gathering mosses, barks, grasses, herbs and fungi to heal and cook with; we had to stop and wait for him on several occasions.

(Not necessarily a bad thing, although Balt was becoming a wee bit impatient.)

Meeka was relieved and happy for Kuchoff, who was clearly feeling his best as he was running around, chasing small animals like squirrels and rabbits.

Kuchoff was helping Loher, for as he would scare up some game, the elven maiden would pick them off with her bow and arrows, saving the meat for future meals.

(We were all quite tired of fish, as that is all it seems we had eaten for weeks.)

I have a feeling that the sailors the captain had brought along were enjoying their time on land; I did not see even the hint of a frown on either of their faces, nor that of the captain's as well, although it was clear to all that he was still upset about the state of his ship – rightly so.

As a matter of fact, Balt looked to be enjoying himself as he and Kuchoff were becoming fast friends, the elder of the two donating much of his attention to the younger with that of an uncle's interest.

Brother Fost had finally gathered all that he could and after meticulously placing each sample in its own bag and gingerly placing each bag in a well-organized pack, we moved along a few meters until he discovered a new sample that he wanted to gather; moments later, we finally arrived at the edge of the clearing.

Both Meeka and Loher gasped at the sheer beauty of the clearing, and I must admit that I too was awe-stricken once I saw it in daylight.

Balt was obviously itching to go in and explore, as was the captain.

"Can either of you feel or sense anything magical or otherwise pertaining to the clearing?" I asked Meeka and Kuchoff.

After several minutes, Meeka reported that she felt that it was safe to cautiously proceed.

Kuchoff on the other hand, was silent; he was sitting on the ground, cross legged with his eyes closed and breathing in a rhythmic pattern.

We all stood there, watching him, with slight anticipation.

After several minutes of watching Kuchoff focus, and Balt slowly lose patience, Kuchoff finally opened his eyes and reported that the clearing was recently endowed with magic but was rapidly becoming naturally neutral.

"Is anyone or anything alive in there?" Byron asked.

Kuchoff stood up, stretched and nodded his head in affirmation with a quiet yawn.

"Did ye 'av a guid sleep, Boy-o?" Balt asked with a chuckle.

⁕

As soon as the team entered the clearing, the scenery suddenly changed.

The landscape stayed the same, but now, there were structures and tents where there were none before.

We must have entered into some sort of magical cloaking dome created by whoever lives in the structures in order to keep the village hidden...or so I was assuming.

This came to us as a shock, so we readied our weapons and Byron whispered for us to get down and take cover.

From my 'mouse's-eye' point of view, crouched in the tall grass, I could see that the huts and houses were extremely small, old and run down as if abandoned, while the tents were weathered but still in fairly good shape and about the usual size that an elf, or human would use.

The tiny houses and huts were scattered about the clearing in no certain pattern.

Except for one, larger house set somewhat in the center of the clearing.

The tents were strategically placed, making a wide circle around three larger tents in the center of the clearing; the tent in the very center was quite a bit larger than the other two, set right near the largest tiny house.

I was almost convinced that no one was around until I saw slight movement near one of the smaller tents.

My companions saw my sudden dip down lower, so they followed suit and looked toward me as if to ask, 'what did you see?'

I pointed in the direction of the movement.

Byron, Balt and Captain Waxx's gazes followed my fingertip.

After a moment, each of my companions, one by one, dipped back down into the tall grass.

(Balt really didn't have that far to go.)

The movement turned out to be some kind of humanoid creature, (I couldn't make out any features,) that swiftly moved from one of the smaller tents circling the clearing, to the largest tent in the center.

We needed to regroup and come up with a better plan.

Several minutes went by with no sight of any movement, so we slowly made our way back to our path in the woods.

"We are definitely not alone on this island," Loher stated dramatically.

Balt suddenly slapped his own forehead and gave Loher a wide-eyed look, "Really Lass?" He grunted sarcastically, "I dinna notice."

Loher balled up her fist and almost began to lean into a punch, but then remembered that she had almost been sarcastic toward him not long ago and decided to just accept it and move on.

"I suggest we talk 'bout dis in de camp, Mon," the captain announced, "an be post'n extra guards in de night-time."

I nodded in agreement and led the team back to the ship.

Once we arrived on the beach, Captain Waxx asked for volunteers to help stand watch at night, picked out a few men and sent them off to get some rest, "I be need'n you wide awake an ready to fight, Bruddahs," he told them.

The men agreed respectfully and then disappeared into the ship.

"Did anyone get a clear view of what that creature was?" I asked.

Balt just shook his head.

"Sorry, Mon," the captain regretfully answered.

"Byron?" I coaxed.

"I'm not sure what I saw," he reported, "it was too tall to be a dwarf or halfling and I could plainly see that it wasn't human or elf." He paused, thinking for a moment and then spat out in frustration, "I'm not sure what I saw."

"We needs ta git back in t'ere and s'plore," Balt grunted, obviously disappointed that we retreated to regroup.

"We have no idea what we're up against," Meeka rhetorically explained.

"Or how many," Kuchoff added.

"'Ow de ye tink me ancestors got so far in life, eh?" Balt spat, "Na by sittin' on our arses and bein' sissies."

"And how many dwarves are left to talk about it?" Loher quietly defended.

The wizard began to smile in agreement with the elven maiden as Balt took a breath, raised a finger and began to campaign.

I cleared my throat to gain the attention, "I think I have a plan that will make everyone happy; Balt, probably not as much, but still happy."

All eyes were finally on me.

I suddenly felt as if the weight of the world was set upon my shoulders.

Without saying a word, I simply put the hood of my invisibility cloak over my head and stood silent.

I could see my companions just as well as I could a moment before, but as I put my hood up, the rest of the team began to look confused and lose focus, as if they were looking past where I was standing just seconds later, one by one, beginning with the Priest, they understood that I had just disappeared as I was wearing the Invisibility Cloak that I had found in the Monere Tower.

"I remember when you found that cloak," Brother Fost giggled.

A few of the others nodded in agreement.

"That will come in handy," Loher stated as she too raised her own hood and vanished as well.

We lowered our hoods and reappeared where we once were.

"I guess it's settled," Byron laughed, "you two go in and scout."

Captain Waxx smiled and agreed.

"Where kin I git me one o' tose?" Balt commented with a slight tone of unhappiness.

"I always thought dwarves didn't trust magic," Byron stated.

Balt shot him a look of distaste and quietly grumbled something in Dwarven.

Loher and I gathered up our gear and along with the small team of Balt, Byron and the two large sailors, we began to head back down the path to the clearing.

CHAPTER THREE

INVITUS

We arrived at the clearing, and I could swear that I could hear my heartbeat from inside my chest.

"Can you hear that?" I outwardly asked.

My companions stopped and listened.

"Hear what?" Byron asked, confused, "the birds?"

I shook my head and waited for another answer.

The sailors both shook their heads as well.

"I hear nutt'n outta ta ordinary," Balt agreed.

I smiled, shrugged and acted as if it was nothing to be concerned about.

All attention was turned to the clearing.

"Are you ready to go in?" Loher asked and reached for her hood.

"As ready as I'll ever be," I answered and pulled my hood over my head, "after all, this was my idea."

Oddly enough, as I pulled on my hood, I noticed that I could still see Loher and I could tell by her reaction that she too could still see me.

"Can you see us?" Loher and I asked at the same time.

Our companions simultaneously looked around and answered, "No."

"I can see you, Loher," I admitted.

"I can see you as well," Loher replied.

"I wonder if we will be able to see other invisible objects," I rhetorically commented.

"Perhaps ye will," Balt supposed, "go in tere and find out!" He coaxed impatiently and reached out to push us toward the clearing, but only found empty space.

"Be careful," Byron commanded.

I habitually made a gesture of agreement and then realized that he didn't see it, so I grabbed Loher's arm and escorted her into the clearing and into the magical dome that masked the village within.

Loher showed little to no surprise as the huts and tents suddenly appeared once we entered the unseen dome.

I began to crouch down, not used to the fact of being invisible, but Loher pulled me back up with a slight giggle and smiled.

It was a slight comfort, knowing that I could not be seen except for by someone else that was obscured as well.

Loher and I slowly began to make our way to the closest tent.

As we traveled, Loher kept an eye out for trip wires and other traps while I kept an eye out for various tracks and markings.

We both kept an eye out for whoever it was that was occupying this clearing.

Our concealment must have been doing its job well, because we slowly crept past a group of ground roosting birds without disturbing them; I felt quite satisfied and significantly calmer and more confident.

As we reached the closest tent, we looked inside and discovered a small cache of bladed weapons; we decided to leave it alone... for now.

There were also two quite comfortable looking circular bunks that looked recently slept in, as well as the remains of a small cooking fire near the mouth of the tent.

We decided to go from tent to tent to determine how many creatures there were and how well they were armed.

A few tents later, we decided that they should all be the same, as the few we already explored were quite similar: two bunks, a cold fire ring and a cache of weapons.

We were surprised and a bit concerned yet grateful that we had not run into any of whoever these 'people' were, friend or foe.

Where are they?

Who are they?

What are they??

It was obvious to us that there were more than two dozen of these creatures residing here.

Our next objectives were the tents in the center, beginning with the closest mid-sized one.

As we approached the tent, we began to hear voices within the tent.

Fortunately, and very surprisingly, they were speaking an archaic dialect of Elven; that of the ancient half elven race called the Elrohir Melwasul.

The elrohir melwasul were an experimental breed of soldier comprised of both elven and feline genes.

Known for their exceptional skills of tracking and stalking as well as enhanced speed, they were a formidable assassin breed used for covert operations.

Just as tall as full-blooded elves, but bulkier, weighing slightly more due to the extra muscle mass, their features resembled more of an elf than that of a feline, except for the prominent markings in their hair and subtle markings on their variously color tinted skin depending on the breed of feline they were mixed with.

Their skin, covered with a very short, very fine fur, some were an orangish tint while others had more of a darker complexion, and some were even as pale as snow.

Narrower faces that brought their eyes closer together gave them the advantage of better depth perception and sight distance, their teeth resembled those of a large feline and their ears were a bit larger and set a bit higher on their heads.

Their voices were deeper than that of a pure elf, and featured a melodic feline-like quality, while their mannerisms as well, were more graceful, elegant and almost leisurely in nature.

Unfortunately, their natural life span was only less than half of a pure-bred elf, but almost double that of a human.

According to elven history, the elrohir melwasul, or 'Eline,' the name that they had given to themselves, had successfully served their purpose and were no longer needed so they were discontinued.

Those living were allowed to live out their years in peace among the elves, but procreation was strictly prohibited under penalty of death.

Until now, I had always believed that they had gone extinct.

Loher and I looked at each other with a mixture of shock, excitement and fear.

I suggested by pointing at the path that we go back to the ship and come up with a better plan; Loher agreed.

———— ◆ ————

We began to back away from the tent when suddenly an eline emerged from the opening.

We froze.

There, standing directly before us, was a legendary eline.

It was mostly light orange and yellow with bold black and brown stripe-like markings about its face and what we could see of the body, beyond the padded leather and semi banded armor it wore.

An obvious warrior, recognizable not only by the armor it wore, but also by the large, well-crafted sword on its belt.

It looked around and sniffed the air.

We were fortunately standing down wind or we would have been discovered for sure.

It stopped sniffing and looked directly at us, blinked a few times and then proceeded away from the tent.

We still stood frozen in place and watched as it disappeared into one of the smaller tents.

As soon as it was out of sight, we decided to make a break for it and get back to the ship to warn the others.

We didn't make it very far.

Before I could even venture a guess about what had happened, it was over even quicker.

I found myself pinned to the ground by an eline; Loher was pinned by another, and I could see two more standing nearby.

"I could have killed you," my grey and black striped captor said with a smile.

"Why didn't you?" I boldly asked.

"Why didn't you?" My captor mimicked, "You smell like elves, and we don't kill elves..." he answered, "...right away."

"We are very curious about who you are," Loher's almost pure white captor breathed, "and how you got here."

"And why?" my captor completed.

"Then our aims are mutual," I audaciously replied and relaxed.

Loher and I were yanked to our feet, hoods off, stripped of our weapons and led to the largest center tent.

Once inside the tent, we were told to sit and explain ourselves.

"I have a better idea," I stated, "I'll make you a deal…"

"You're in no position to make deals," one of the eline warned.

"I'd like to hear his idea," another commented.

The apparent leader of the four eline, also orangish yellow with brown and black striped markings only darker in color and physically much larger, gestured me to go ahead.

"I propose," I began, "that we answer a question, then you answer one of our questions, then we answer, then you answer and so on."

The leader thought about my suggestion for a moment and then agreed, "We take turns."

"Fair is fair," I offered, "You ask first."

"Who are you?" The leader asked.

"My name is Thunor McLaaud, and this is Loher D'Rolwynn; we are both from Laryx in the Seolfer Wudu."

The leader nodded, "I have heard of that place," he paused, "stories were passed down from generation to generation."

"I never believed that they were true," another eline commented.

It was my turn to ask, "Who are all of you?"

The leader spoke first, "I am called Cirdan Telrunya, my second in command is Huor Eledhwen, and my third is called Lamalas Anwamane and his friend Mablung Nenmacil, all from Nargothrond."

"Never heard of it," I admitted.

I came to realize that it was Mablung that we saw earlier, coming out of the tent before we ran; he must have been going to Lamalas' tent.

Huor was my captor while Lamalas captured Loher.

"How many more are there in your party?" Cirdan asked.

I didn't feel comfortable telling our new 'friends' the full truth, so I lied, "five more at camp."

Not a complete lie if I didn't include the pirates.

Loher shot me a look of approval.

"I know that there are more here than just you four," I began, "how many?"

Cirdan puffed out his chest and proudly announced, "I am in command of twenty-six eline."

'That makes things about even,' I thought to myself, 'if it wasn't for their enhanced abilities.'

"Your turn," I commented.

"Why are you here on this island?" Cirdan probed.

"Do you remember that storm that ripped through here yesterday?" I asked, but before anyone could answer, I continued, "Our ship was caught in that storm and crashed onto some rocks here on this island," I stopped and took a breath, "what about you? Why are you here?"

"Storm?" Cirdan asked, "I recall no storm, not even a light rain."

"Perhaps it was on the far edge of the island," Mablung suggested.

Cirdan quickly turned and looked at Lamalas and pointed at Mablung, "Get him out of here!" He roared, "All of you...LEAVE!"

The three eline nodded respectfully and evacuated the tent.

Cirdan looked at me with an extremely serious look on his face, "You will lead a group of my men to your ship when we are through with our questions."

"Are you going to answer my question?" I boldly asked.

"That is classified information," Cirdan recited.

"Well, you might as well tell us," I coaxed, "if you're not going to kill us, we'll eventually figure it out anyway."

"As you wish," Cirdan conceded with a grin full of sharp fang-like teeth, "We were hired by the Grand Ascendancy to secure this island by massacring the native inhabitants," he then suddenly looked down as if shamed.

"You don't seem eager to do it though," I coaxed.

"No," he admitted, "I'm having a difficult time justifying the slaughter of an entire race of innocent, yet extremely magical creatures for a power-hungry faction that abuses magic," he paused and then looked up with an evil glint in his eyes and laughed, "Magic. A trait that we should have inherited from our elven ancestors but didn't."

"My companions and I can help you," I half soothed while also trying to save our skins.

"How can seven elves help us against the Grand Ascendancy?" He laughed again.

He had been open and honest with us, so I decided to give a bit of honesty back, "Two elves, a dwarf, a halfling and about two hundred humans, two of which are wizards."

"You told me that there were only seven of you!" Cirdan roared angrily.

I smiled and raised a single finger into the air, "You asked me how many were in my party," I defended, "the captain and his crew are not part of my party; therefore, I didn't lie."

Cirdan stood there for a moment with his teeth still bared at me, eyes locked onto mine as if to intimidate me.

I began to smile when I watched a string of drool collect and then drop from his fangs.

"Fair enough," he blinked and reluctantly gave in as he noticed my smile, "but even six hundred humans wouldn't match the power of the Grand Ascendancy."

"What is The Grand Ascendancy?" I finally asked.

Cirdan stopped and thought for a moment and then admitted, "We don't really know much about them, other than that they're powerful wizards lead by an even more powerful sorceress or something similar, in control of a large army of beasts that are, for some reason, willing to do anything, and I mean anything for them." He paused, "And they have a lot of money."

"If they have this great army," Loher spoke, "Why did they hire you?"

The catlike warrior narrowed his eyes at her, "Orcs and hobgoblins are stupid and are only good for fighting... poorly at best, but they're cheap and easy to feed. We get the job done." He paused and laughed, "Until now, apparently."

"Have you actually **met** any of them?" I asked.

"Oh, yes," he purred, "only a few of the foot soldiers...err...wizards."

"You seem pleased by that," Loher noted.

"Up until recently, we were allies and I enjoyed the company of most of those I knew," he frowned, "I miss one in particular greatly."

"I am personal friends with Lagu Ofer'Eal, reigning King of all Beornan Heafod..." I began.

"We're not in Beornan Heafod, if you hadn't noticed," He cut me off as he slumped into his chair; "Your king is nothing here."

The tent was filled with utter silence for quite some time.

Sounds of the eline soldiers training could be heard in the distance.

The sound of a blacksmith could barely be heard, even further away.

I wondered if it was Balt, or someone else.

I began to miss my horse, Stahvee.

"How do we get back?" I rhetorically moaned under my breath.

"Magic," He simply answered after a moment.

I thought about the situation at hand for a few moments and then it hit me, "Perhaps the magical creatures that you were sent here to kill would be able to help us!? Help all of us, with both of our situations!"

"That's not a bad idea except for the fact that we're trying to kill them!" He roared.

"My companions and I aren't." I quietly corrected with a defiant smirk.

Cirdan slowly relaxed his clenched jaw and looked at me with a blank look on his oddly featured face, stared at me for a few more seconds and then dropped his head back down, sulking, "How do I know that I can trust you?" He finally asked, still not completely sure.

"We're racially related, aren't we?" I cunningly asked.

"Your race tried to condemn and exterminate us," He countered.

"You've been hired to do the same to the people of this land," I calmly parried.

"You manufactured us." Cirdan jabbed, obviously reaching for an argument yet, somehow, calmer now.

"Not my fault," I feigned a laugh, "that was over two lifetimes ago, and I had no part in that," I argued, "besides, like you, I am only half elf."

He looked up at me again and studied my face, this time with a glint back in his eyes and a half smile upon his face, "There will be dire consequences if you cheat me," he warned.

"The sentiment is mutual," Loher murmured.

Cirdan only looked at her with confusion in his eyes.

"As if the same wouldn't be true if the roles were reversed," I translated.

"Come then," he said, eyeing us up and down once more, "I'll escort you to the edge of the clearing and inform my men that we are allies... for now. I still don't completely trust you."

"The sentiment is mutual," Loher echoed.

———◆———

We were handed back our weapons before we followed Cirdan out of the tent and into one of the mid-sized tents.

This tent was filled with several eline leaning over a large table covered in maps.

Weapons: more weapons than I had ever seen in one area lined the walls.

"You see those weapons?" Cirdan chuckled and splayed his hand around the room, "they're useless against the errfords."

"Errfords?" Loher asked.

"The native species of the island," Cirdan answered.

"Are they thick skinned or armored?" She continued, as if she was conducting an interview.

Cirdan laughed aloud, "No, they're very small and furry."

We both gave him an obvious look of disbelief.

"You're joking," we accused together.

"Seriously," Cirdan nervously laughed, "It's true, they are."

"And your weapons are useless against them?" I asked.

"Even a bow?" Loher added.

"These weapons are useless against their magic," he answered, a clawed finger held in the air, becoming serious, "we have tried everything we could think of, even bows, and we still can't kill even one of their weakest."

"How do you know which are the weakest?" Loher asked.

"We don't," Cirdan admitted, "we only assumed that the smaller or elderly would be the weaker."

"In some species," Loher argued, "the elderly are the strongest, due to wisdom and experience."

"That's true," Cirdan agreed becoming confused and frustrated at the situation, "but—"

Loher cut him off, frustrating the commander even more, "And in other species, like venomous snakes," Loher smiled, amused at the eline's frustration, "the smaller are the more deadly, due to the concentrated venom, which gets weaker the older the snake gets. I bet you didn't know that."

"I thought you said that you didn't want to kill them?" I inquired, trying to end the argument.

Loher shot me a pained look as I spoiled her fun.

"We don't," he responded, "but it's starting to feel like she's trying to kill me," he nervously chuckled, nodding at Loher.

Loher smiled slyly and shifted her weight on her feet.

"This situation is just one of the reasons that we became averse to killing them in the first place," Cirdan sighed, "And they won't fight back, so it's not even any fun."

Cirdan walked up to one of the soldiers that was studying a map and told him to gather a few men for a simple escort assignment.

The soldier agreed and exited the tent; we slowly followed his path and exited the tent as well.

Suddenly, out of the corner of my eye, I noticed Balt and one of the sailors, creeping through the tall grass.

"We have company," I half laughed, "our companions decided to send out a search party."

"Your men are smart," Cirdan complimented.

I looked toward the dwarf and sailor, showing the eline where to look.

Cirdan followed my gaze and spotted the team, "I can see you!" He shouted cordially.

Balt and the sailor stopped.

No movement, no sound.

"You don't have to hide!" I called.

No movement, no sound.

"They're friends!" I called again.

"Dammit!" I heard Balt curse as he and the sailor got up and began walking toward us.

(I could see the sailor very well; Balt, however, was still hidden by the taller grass by no fault of his own.)

The dwarf and sailor finally arrived at the mouth of the tent, and I could see Balt eyeing Cirdan up and down.

He was gathering information about this new potential foe that he had never encountered before, like, what were the possible weak points of this creature?

What advantages does it have over me?

What advantages do I have over it?

Balt was a cunning warrior due to this system.

"Wot is it?" The dwarf asked me, pointing a thumb at Cirdan.

"An ancient race of elven kind that we thought were extinct for thousands of years," I explained, "they are called, elrohir melwasul and his name is Cirdan."

"We prefer the name, Eline." Cirdan corrected.

Balt eyed Cirdan up and down one more time as Cirdan obviously did the same.

"How is it that you travel together?" Cirdan asked out of curiosity.

"Tat be a long story," Balt grumbled, "best left fer a-nutter time."

Cirdan looked at me with a confused look on his face; all I could do was smile in an apologetic way.

Four armed eline soldiers marched up to us and reported for their escort assignment; they were being led by Huor Eledhwen.

"Reporting as ordered, Sir," Huor formally stated.

"You will escort these people back to their ship and verify that they are here due to a shipwreck," Cirdan ordered, "as well as the number of approximately two hundred crew and seven passengers; go unarmed, this is a peaceful mission."

"As you command," Huor formally regurgitated, "Stow your weapons," he ordered the other soldiers, "and report back here at once!"

The soldiers scrambled back to their tents and then one by one returned unarmed.

"Lead the way," Huor offered.

We escorted the eline that were supposed to be escorting us, (confused yet?) to the path and met up with Byron and the other large sailor.

"We were getting concerned when you didn't come back," Byron stated as he too, eyed up the eline soldiers.

"We made new friends," I said, exaggerating a smile, "we are being escorted back to the ship."

"Is that so?" Byron asked, making sure I wasn't trying to warn him of a trap.

"Seriously," I smiled again and 'rested' my hand on the hilt of my sword.

Byron looked and noticed that the soldiers were unarmed; he relaxed a bit and he and the other sailor joined our parade.

We announced ourselves as we approached the camp and were met by Brother Fost, armed with his Blessed Crossbow.

I heard a few of the eline soldiers hiss out muffled giggles at the sight of the tiny halfling and his equally tiny crossbow.

Brother Fost grimaced and bared his teeth at the offenders.

The guilty were made to apologize before they could enter the camp.

"Go ahead," I offered the eline soldiers. "Look around."

Meeka and Captain Waxx approached me from different directions, "What's going on?" Meeka whispered.

I waited for Captain Waxx to catch up and then explained the situation.

As I explained, I looked around and noticed that the repairs to The Scorpion were in the final finishing stages, but it was still quite obvious that the ship had been recently repaired.

The eline soldiers noticed it too and took notes.

They also performed an approximate head count and saw that I had told the truth.

Apparently satisfied with their findings, they left the same way we had arrived, without saying a word.

As soon as they were gone, Loher and I were bombarded with questions, so we called a circle meeting and attempted to answer them all.

Our conference lasted well into the evening and almost into the night.

One important topic that Meeka wanted to discuss was what she found in that strange tome she had found on the body of the dead wizard.

"Are you ready for this?" Meeka asked with an excited smile, "That sect of wizards is called..."

"The Grand Ascendancy," I smiled, cutting her off.

She only blinked at me with confusion written all over her face.

"Cirdan told us as much as he could about them, but it wasn't much."

"I'll keep studying," Meeka informed as she began to turn to walk away.

"By the way," Loher advised, "they may not all be wizards."

"What do you mean?" Meeka inquired.

"Cirdan mentioned that they are magically powerful, but never confirmed if they're all wizards. He used the term, 'similar to wizards' but wasn't specific."

Meeka nodded and strode away to study what clues she had.

We had also decided to continue repairing the ship and as soon as it was done, we would inform Cirdan, find out where the errfords were hiding and attempt to make peaceful contact with them.

⊷◉⊶

The Scorpion rocked gently on the small waves in the cove we found near where we had crashed.

It had been almost a year until the repairs were completed, but the ship was finally safely anchored offshore.

It wasn't even a full day when we were (unexpectedly) visited by Huor and a small attachment of eline soldiers.

"Cirdan requests an audience with you," he informed me politely.

"Is that a nice way of telling me that I'm ordered to report to him?" I jokingly asked and looked over at Kuchoff who was also giggling.

"Yes," he answered in a serious tone.

Kuchoff stopped giggling.

"Did he tell you who to bring back?" I asked, feigning a smile.

"Yes," he answered, still seriously, "he ordered me to retrieve you."

"Only me?" No smile.

"Yes." No smile.

'If this is a trap or trick of some sort,' I thought to myself, 'we wouldn't be leaving the rest of my team and two hundred sailors behind as a rescue party.'

I also noticed that the eline were unarmed again, which further eased my mind, but I kept my weapons.

Kuchoff suddenly ran up to me, "Take me with you... Dad," he cried.

The young man had a strange look in his eyes and was not showing off his usual toothy grin, besides the fact that he had never called me 'Dad' before, I decided to play along.

"Is it okay if I bring my kid?" I asked.

Huor agreed, "Just make it quick."

"We're ready to go now," I announced. "Let's go."

Loher and Meeka had looks of concern on their faces, while Balt just looked angrier than a bored hornet that he wasn't going along.

I had a feeling that he would attempt to follow us as soon as we were out of sight.

Balt always had my back, whether I needed it or not.

Besides, Kuchoff was his best friend and I'm sure he would worry about him more than he would worry about me.

I trusted Kuchoff, and if he felt that he needed to come with me; so be it.

His strange Psi powers were something I still don't completely understand, but I trusted them.

He had gotten us out of quite a few scrapes by using them.

Sadly, the journey to the clearing was uneventful, I had hoped for some idle talk, but soldiers, especially eline, are trained to be silent.

Their command structure reminded me a bit of the way Lagu Ofer'Eal wanted things done in his kingdom; it was relaxed, yet still formal when needed.

When we arrived at the command tent, the first question Cirdan asked was, "Why does your son look so...human?"

I thought quickly, "His mother is full human, and I am half human, so he looks more human than we expected."

Kuchoff feigned a hurt look, to make it look a bit more convincing.

"The other children teased me," Kuchoff added.

Cirdan leaned down and leveled himself with the young man, "how old are you, Kid?"

"Twelve, in a few days," Kuchoff answered honestly.

"I was teased by the other children as well," he straightened up, "when I was a child."

"Were you different?" Kuchoff asked.

"I grew up around elves, four or five humans and the other eline," he stated, "we eline all were teased by most of the full elf and a few of the human children... until we got older."

"What happened then?" Kuchoff asked, eyes wide, leaning in.

Cirdan smiled slyly, "We eline were much stronger and faster than all of the others, so they learned to fear...err...respect us."

Kuchoff nodded in understanding, intently gazing at the eline commander.

"Tell me boy," Cirdan inquired, "do you have any... magical abilities from your elven ancestry?"

Kuchoff smiled and nodded his head.

Cirdan frowned a bit, "Show me?"

Kuchoff looked up at me as if asking permission.

I nodded approval, "Something simple."

Kuchoff smiled his usual toothy grin and raised his right hand in front of him about shoulder high.

Suddenly, under his hand, the dust and dirt on the floor inside of the tent began to swirl into a mini tornado, complete with lightning and thunder.

"I have to admit," Cirdan spoke as the tornado dissipated, "I am a bit jealous of you."

"Why?" Kuchoff asked.

"We eline are half elf and half feline and we didn't get any magical abilities, while you are only a quarter elf, and you did."

"That seems unfair to me too," Kuchoff consoled; an attempt to strengthen the alliance between the eline and us.

Cirdan looked fondly upon the boy for a moment and then snapped back into seriousness once again, "I asked you here because I understand that your ship is seaworthy again, am I correct?"

"Indeed, you are," I agreed.

"Ahh, good," he smiled, "it is time for you to encounter the errfords."

CHAPTER FOUR

CONVENTUS INNOCENTIUM MALUM

To me, looking at the maps that the eline had gathered was about as useful as a bow with no string, but to Brother Fost, they were priceless!

Somehow, probably with his Psi skills, Kuchoff had completely assured Cirdan that we can be trusted and a few days later, we had moved camp to the clearing to keep a closer eye on our new...friends; Captain Waxx had a revolving skeleton crew stay aboard The Scorpion.

When the eline first arrived on this island, it only took them a few days to find and attempt to destroy the errford creatures, but they failed and the errfords got away and hid on another part of the island.

Locating a magical dome that keeps an entire population of creatures invisible was proving to be difficult, although the dome that we were occupying was fading.

We noticed that we were beginning to be able to see the tents from outside the dome when we were returning from a hunt.

The dome's fading was of no real concern to us, but it gave us only a taste of how magically powerful the errford really were.

The eline had already occupied the dome for a few weeks before we showed up and it was only then that the residual magic was beginning to weaken to the point of becoming transparent enough to barely see through.

None of this really means anything for the hunt; I just thought it was an interesting observance.

On one hand, their magic is apparently so strong that they could almost certainly return us back to our own realm, but on the other hand, it may be so powerful that one of them could just sneeze and wipe us all out of existence.

Regardless, we had to try to make contact with them and convince them to help us.

We had already sailed all the way around the island, which took just under three days, due to its immense size.

From the water, the island looked to be mid-sized, almost small, but when you get right up close to it, it gets bigger and bigger; almost massive.

We searched and found nothing; no sign of errford life.

We even started at one end of the island with a long line of people clasping hands and tried to do a sweep of the entire area, but the foliage was so thick in most places, that we would have had to strip the entire island in order to make it through: not conventional or nature friendly, and our attempt took a full two weeks until we decided to give up.

We also tried having Kuchoff psionically scan the island as we sailed around it, but his energy drained too quickly, and we refused to risk his health by continuing to do it.

We were running out of ideas and options, but we needed to do something; we had to form a strategy of some kind, like a methodical search pattern.

Time seemed to be quickly passing as each of our ideas were tried and failed.

Meeka even decided to conjure up a large mischief of magical mice, (like the mouse that she used to impress us when we first met,) and send them off in all directions to see if they could find the errford location, but each were eaten by predators.

She said that the first few deaths were quite horrifying to experience firsthand, so she withdrew the spell.

Day after day, we would come up with a new idea, day after day we would try our new ideas and day after day, each and every one of our new ideas would utterly fail.

Another year went by as we tried each new technique until...

———— ◆ ————

Loher took a moment to steady herself and get a good aim on the deer, half hidden within the ferns.

She took a deep breath and relaxed her fingers.

Silently, her bowstring snapped forward, releasing the arrow, thrusting it forward toward its target; it glided through the air...

Suddenly and inexplicably, the arrow veered upward and struck a large dead branch, dislodging it from its former home, allowing gravity to take a hold and smash it down...

A wild, high-pitched scream erupted from under the downed branch.

Loher, Byron and I cautiously approached where the piercing sound was emanating from.

Trapped under the fallen branch, was a creature that we had never seen the likes of before.

It was about the size of a common gray squirrel, only with long, puffy reddish-brown fur, but there was also something very odd about it.

As a team, we prepared to capture it in hopes that this was, in fact, an errford.

"On the count of three," I proposed, "one, two, three!"

Loher produced a suitably sized leather sack from her pack, while Byron lifted the dead branch from the creature, and I attempted to grab the creature and quickly transfer it into the sack.

Our plan succeeded; creature nabbed.

We decided to bring the creature back to camp.

Brother Fost would know what to do.

Cirdan was confused, "Tell me again, how you captured this errford?"

This was the third time I had to explain it to him; he was in slight shock that something so simple could have done it.

The creature was odd.

We had no time to really look at it when we captured it.

Small, about the size (like I said before) of a common gray squirrel with long puffy reddish-brown fur all over except for its hands and face.

Its hands closely resembled ours; instead of paws and claws, it had four fingers and an opposable thumb.

Its face resembled ours as well; there was nothing rodent-like about it.

Just looking at the errford's face almost made me believe that it could speak.

"I have a theory," Brother Fost announced and pulled me out of my daydream.

"Let's hear it." I replied.

Loher, you were aiming at a deer, correct?" The priest asked in order to validate his thoughts.

"Yes," Loher confirmed.

"Good," he smiled, "and the arrow suddenly changed direction to an upward angle?"

"Yes."

"Mmm hmm," the priest murmured with his fingers stroking his chin, deep in thought, "like it struck a rock and was deflected?"

"But there was no rock," Loher disputed, "It was a clear sh—"

Brother Fost held up his hand and cut her off, "Yes or no, Loher, like it struck a rock..."

"Well, yes, but there—" she began again.

"The arrow," the priest emphasized sharply in order to drown out the voice of the elven maiden, "then struck a dead branch and said branch fell down and trapped this errford, correct?"

"Yes."

Cirdan cut in, "Our weapons have no effect on the errford."

"Loher," Brother Fost continued, ignoring the eline, "can you lead me to the exact place that this happened?"

"Certainly," Loher agreed.

"My theory is," Brother Fost announced, "that the branch fell on and trapped the errford so easily, because... the errford was more concerned with you, and saving the life of the deer, than it was about the arrow that it had magically deflected... upward... the arrow in turn, struck the branch making it fall; now, the errford had no idea that said branch was coming down to trap it, so... it didn't magically deflect the branch, hence the branch trapping it, consequently stunning it temporarily, allowing you to capture it," he paused, "do you understand?"

"Yes," we all said in synchronicity.

"So," Brother Fost continued, "in theory, where there was one, more, perhaps even their new home, should be close by."

"I have a question," I stated.

"Yes, Thunor?" The priest entertained.

"If these errford are so magically powerful, why and how do we still have it captured?" I asked, "If it is so powerful, why doesn't it just... 'magic' its way out of here?"

"I shall ponder..." the priest began and then drifted into deep thought.

After several minutes of semi-silence, "We can't control it," a tiny, frightened voice announced in broken Halfling.

"I knew it!" I exclaimed as I whipped around and looked at the errford, "I knew that you could talk!"

"What do you mean, you can't control it?" Loher gently asked, so as not to frighten it any more than it already was.

After some hesitation, the errford spoke again, this time in Elven, "Our gifts only surface in times of need," it explained, "for protection or healing and such."

"Do you have a name?" I asked, trying to keep the creature engaged.

"I am called Gig," it answered, again in mixed Human and Elven.

"Are you male or female?" Loher asked, testing a theory.

"Male," Gig answered in complete Elven.

She wasn't satisfied with a one worded answer, so she asked, "What were you doing out there, away from the rest of your kind?"

Gig answered again in complete Elven, confirming Loher's suspicion that the errford, or at least this one, empathize with everyone that he interacts with; Gig answered, "I was about to gather food, my pantry is almost empty."

"That's amazing," Loher smiled, "Balt," she said, "ask him a question."

"Do wot?"

"Ask Gig a question."

The dwarf stood there thinking for a moment, "Are ye scared, wee one?"

"I am more frightened for the welfare of my family once I meet my final fate," he boldly answered in complete Dwarven.

"What did he say?" I asked, not understanding a word of Dwarven.

Balt repeated the errford's words, adding with a chuckle, "I like ta wee lad, he gots guts."

Cirdan finally spoke up, "Gig, we would like to speak to your leader, if you have one, is that possible?"

"Do what you will with me, Monster, but I'll never betray my tribe!" Gig spat back in Eline.

With Gig's final word, an orb of pure energy erupted from around his body and raced toward Cirdan's head.

Cirdan ducked away just in time, avoiding the orb, which slammed into the wall of the tent and burned a hole clear through.

Two armed eline soldiers immediately entered the tent with weapons ready, but Cirdan quickly held up a hand and dismissed them without a word.

Cirdan feigned a smile and calmly said, "We are not going to kill you, or anyone else in your tribe, we just need to speak to your leader," he opened the makeshift cage that held Gig captive, "it is very important."

"**Liar!**" Gig roared in Eline.

Cirdan flinched at the sudden outburst and jumped back a few feet.

"He's not lying, Gig," I countered.

"Why is it so important?" Gig asked defiantly.

"Each of our lives," Brother Fost began, "including those of your tribe, are in grave danger and we need your tribe's help to make it safe again."

"I still don't believe you!" Gig spat; his body once again began to glow.

Cirdan put his hands up in a slight surrendering pose, "The Grand Ascendancy hired my soldiers and me to exterminate you," Cirdan admitted, "but we are refusing to do so, because I cannot justify the extermination of an innocent race that has no conflict with anyone."

"And now," I continued for him, "when the Grand Ascendancy finds out that their hired assassins are refusing to destroy you, they are going to be very angry and destroy the whole island."

"Why do they want to exterminate us?" Gig asked with fear in his voice.

"They want the island," Cirdan explained, "for tactical reasons."

"I don't understand," Gig countered.

"This island is apparently in a good strategic location," Cirdan clarified.

"So, if they want the island, why would they destroy it?" Gig inquired.

"Simple," Balt cut in, "if tey canna 'ave it... no one kin."

"De'ere be enuff room on De Scorpion to fit a whole bunch of you an get us all off de island, Mon," Captain Waxx offered, "if it come down to it."

"And go where?" Cirdan asked, "We have been here a while and have never seen another ship, boat or island. There's nowhere else to go."

A long silent moment passed as Gig sat down on a half-eaten biscuit and began to ponder his predicament...

"The only way that this is going to happen," Gig stipulated as he reached down, snatched up a small handful of biscuit and popped it into his mouth, "is if you let me go and I talk to my Prime Minister about the situation... Alone."

"How do we know that you'll come back?" Cirdan countered.

The errford looked the eline commander directly in the eyes, "You're asking me to trust you with the lives of my entire tribe, even after you tried to kill us on numerous occasions," Gig spelled out. "Is it so hard for you to turn it around and trust me?"

"I have a better idea," a familiar voice announced as dozens of fairies began to appear.

— ◆ —

"Brendt!" Meeka exclaimed as more fairies entered the tent and flitted around.

"The same," the sprite giggled and executed a perfect three-point landing on Balt's helmet, much to the dwarven warrior's chagrin.

Cirdan was busy ducking down and covering his head while the rest of us (all but Balt) held out our hands to give the fairies places to land, which some eagerly accepted.

"Honestly," I began, "I will admit that I am very happy to see you, Brendt."

"Does that make us friends?" The sprite smiled and teased, wiping a non-existent tear from his eye.

Balt grumbled something impossible to make out and swiped his hand across the top of his helmet, which caused the sprite to take temporary flight, just to return to the same place, landing down hard with a stomp of his foot and a conniving grin.

Balt grumbled again, frowned and leaned hard against the table, which in turn made the fairie covered Kuchoff giggle as well.

"What is the meaning of this?" Cirdan growled.

The Fairie Queen perched upon Loher's shoulder, suddenly hissed and shook a finger at the eline commander, "You have caused enough trouble already, Cirdan!"

"Bad kitty!" several fairies whispered around the tent.

"Your Highness!" The eline commander exclaimed in recognition.

I could see that Brendt was having a difficult time keeping a straight face as the eline commander all but cowered away as he bowed to the Fairie Queen in an apologetic manner.

It looked as though the eline commander was groveling to Balt, and Balt was thoroughly enjoying it with a Kuchoffesque toothy grin.

Looks of shock and surprise sprung up on my companions' faces, as well as my own as we watched the Fairie Queen scold the eline commander.

We had never seen the Fairie Queen so angry before.

The Fairie Queen dismissively waved Cirdan off and then sweetly turned to Brendt, "Tell them our idea."

"As we all know, Your Highness," Brendt began, "the Grand Ascendancy is up to something nefarious and obviously made a poor choice by electing the elrohir melwasul to do their dirty work."

"Eline," Cirdan quietly corrected under his breath.

Brendt was enjoying himself as he continued to dig at the eline commander, "Their poor choice is to our advantage as Cirdan here, failed to follow orders, thus saving the errfords from utter annihilation..."

"The idea, Brendt," the Queen impatiently repeated, cutting the sprite off.

"I elect myself to accompany Mr. Gig to his tribe and speak to his chief, assuring cooperation," Brendt finished with a campy bow.

"And I will join you," the Queen insisted.

Brendt blinked in astonishment at the Queen's boldness but remained calm, "I would be honored, Your Highness."

A slight uproar of disagreement arose from a few of the other fairies.

Brother Fost lightly cleared his throat to gain the Queen's attention and spoke only after he received it, "Your Highness, what, pray tell, are we to do in the interim?"

The Fairie Queen's answer was simple and direct, "Prepare for war."

Chapter Five

STERCORE

Brendt and The Fairie Queen suddenly took to the air and came to a rest on the table next to Gig.

Before Cirdan could even begin to react, Brendt and the Queen each took hold of Gig's hands and vanished, leaving the rest of the fairies as well as the rest of us just standing there, looking blankly at each other.

"The Queen instructed you to prepare for war," a few fairies reaffirmed in unison as they too began to disappear, "it would be in your best interest to proceed."

By this time, all but a select few of the fairies had settled in and blended into the surroundings.

I had to strain to see them and if I hadn't even known that they were present, it would have never even crossed my mind to look.

"Look, Fuzzy, I'm gonna be honest wit 'cha," Balt began, looking directly into Cirdan's catlike eyes, "I doon't like ye an' I certainly doon't trust ye..."

Byron cut in, "Right," he coughed, "we trust you about as far as I could throw Balt across this tent."

"Why wud ye even do tat?" The dwarf asked with a pained look on his face.

Byron nervously half smiled, shrugged and then redirected Balt's attention back to Cirdan.

Loher stepped forward and completed Balt's message, "But it looks like our two groups are going to have to work together to achieve this common goal."

"Which is?" Cirdan questioned, obviously confused with the sudden turn of events, "It looks to me like you need us more than we need you."

"That may be so," Brother Fost stepped in, "but you do need us nonetheless."

"I'm curious," a new, feminine voice attended, "what is our common goal, as my husband had just inquired."

We all turned to face the entrance to the tent and observed an eline woman standing there.

She was slightly smaller than Cirdan; much skinnier by far.

She was a pale cream and whitish color with a dark brownish face and piercing blue eyes.

Her forearms and shins (what we could see of them above the tall boots that she wore) were also the same dark brown color.

She was adorned in a flowing, silky, almost transparent gown that matched the color of her eyes.

"Ahh," Cirdan breathed with a flashy smile and a 'come hither' gesture, "this is my wife, Pellicientes."

(Pronounced: Pella Shin Tass)

She effortlessly glided into the tent, passed between Captain Waxx and Byron and then form fitted herself against Cirdan's hip and side as if they were two pieces of the same puzzle.

"Isn't our common goal to defeat the Grand Ascendancy?" Meeka asked, obviously not affected by the spectacle known as Pellicientes.

"Correct," tiny voices sang from hidden places.

"It's obvious what we can do for them," Pellicientes verbally oozed, seductively running her fingers across Cirdan's chest, "but what can they do for us?"

"The kid is quite powerful, My Love," Cirdan cooed, "I have seen what he can do."

"And the others?" She slithered.

Cirdan gently pushed Pellicientes away from him and firmly grasped each of her arms; he looked her in the eyes and soothingly, yet seriously informed her, "don't underestimate our new...friends here," he dropped her arms and turned to face me, "they have plenty to offer."

Pellicientes reached up and grasped her husband's chin, forcefully turning his head to face her, "I suggest that you sharpen your claws before your men start saying that you've gone soft," she said through gritted teeth.

She pushed his face away and effortlessly glided out of the tent.

"Psycho..." A fairie quietly trilled after her from directly behind me.

Cirdan hung his head in depressed defeat, "Perhaps she's right," he said, "maybe I have gone soft."

Loher and I quickly looked at each other and wordlessly agreed that if we were ever going to get back to our realm again, we had to do whatever was necessary to quickly restore Cirdan's confidence.

"Awe, come now Fuzzy," Balt grunted, "all's ye need is a guid battle ta git back inta it."

Perhaps some training exercises would do us all some good," I suggested.

"Speak fer yerself, Mate." Balt grumbled and walked away.

"I'll go gather most of me men," Captain Waxx announced, "and you go grab yours, Mon."

I have been told that the meeting between Brendt, the Fairie Queen, Gig and his chief, Pik, started off badly and didn't show promise of getting any better...

... "How did you get in here?" Prime Minister Pik shouted, "Gig, who are these two foreigners that you have brought into our clandestine sett?"

Prime Minister Pik was well aged and well fed.

Very well fed.

Pik's physical mass was equivalent to approximately a half dozen or so average sized errfords.

As described before, an average errford is comparable to the size of a common gray squirrel; however Prime Minister Pik was almost the size of a turkey.

... "These two are here to help us in exchange for our help," Gig fruitlessly explained, shaken and nervous.

"What do you mean?" The Prime Minister shouted again, growing increasingly frustrated, "What help? With what?"

"Prime Minister," the Fairie Queen began in a calm soothing voice, "if I may explain..." she waited for his reply.

The mere sound of her voice shocked the Prime Minister into awed silence; He waved his portly hand as if to say, 'proceed.'

"Prime Minister Pik," the Fairie Queen petitioned, "no one is here to harm you, including that furry warrior race that mistakenly attacked your village not long ago; they are called Eline."

The Prime Minister attempted to speak, but the Queen quickly raised her finger as if to say, 'wait, there's more,' so he stopped.

"There is also another group of mixed races, mostly human that beached their ship on this island and have befriended the eline warriors; they've convinced them to lay down arms against you in the future."

The Prime Minister looked less confused as he had regained his composure.

He failed at an attempt to sit up in his seat, regardless, he began to speak again, but the Queen expertly cut him off.

"There is a powerful faction of wizards and other magic using individuals, called The Grand Ascendancy that wants this island for tactical purposes; strategically, this island is in a good place."

The Prime Minister had become interested and amused by her story, "Go on," he urged.

"The eline were contracted by the Grand Ascendancy to exterminate your race of people from the face of this island; they are refusing to do so," the Queen paused.

"So where do we errfords fit into this tale?" He asked.

"The mixed human party is from a different realm called Beornan Heafod," she explained, "they would like to return to their own realm and are desperate to do so."

"So..?"

"So, in exchange for them, as well as the eline warriors, helping you defend and defeat The Grand Ascendancy, they ask for your help in returning them home."

Pik cocked his head to one side as if a thought had occurred to him, "And where do you two fit into this equation?"

"While trying to return them from a different realm, our magic somehow was intercepted by The Grand Ascendancy and dropped them here."

"So why don't the two of you just try again?" He suggested.

"We're not strong enough," Brendt finally spoke, "we need your help."

"I don't know you or your species!" Pik argued, becoming impatient due to Brendt's interruption, "You're both foreign to me and so are your friends. Just because your size is comparable to my own and you possess similar abilities, I'm not automatically convinced that I can trust you."

"Is there anything that we can do to gain your trust or make you feel less threatened?" Brendt asked with a low bow.

"Threatened?" Pik chortled, his loose jowls giggling around his chin, "I don't feel threatened and it's your friends that must prove themselves trustworthy, that is, if I agree to help you, which is very doubtful."

"You have nothing to lose and all to gain!" The Fairie Queen melodically induced.

"Again," Pik laughed as he shifted his massive chubbiness in his seat from one cheek to the other, his long bushy tail temporarily brushing his entire face, "how do I know that your story of a...what did you call them...?"

"The Grand Ascendancy, Sir," Gig offered.

"Yes, yes, this Grand Ascendancy..." Pik gurgled, "...how can I be certain that they exist, and this is not some elaborate ruse to lure us out so that warrior race can annihilate us?"

The Fairie Queen straightened her posture and narrowed her eyes and spoke sternly, "Believe me, Prime Minister; if we wanted you dead...you would already be cold and oozing from your seat, more than you are already."

The Prime Minister sat there staring at her with the look of shock upon his plump and shiny face, but then he blinked and cracked a slow smile and began to utter a chuckle; softly at first until it grew strong enough to violently shake every pudgy centimeter of his furry body, "Oh, Your Highness," Pik laughed almost uncontrollably, "it has been such a long time since anyone has spoken to me like that!"

"Like what, Prime Minister?" The Fairie Queen asked in a calmer voice.

"Honestly, boldly, and with conviction," his words were barely recognizable due to the laughter.

"It," she slightly paused, "is how I am," she said solemnly.

"Let me think on this," he snorted jovially, wiping tears from his eyes, "I like you, Your Highness. I'll send for you tomorrow."

The Prime Minister waved his hand in a dismissing gesture and four errford guards appeared from a hallway and escorted Brendt and the Queen from the room and then out to a clearing.

Laughing and a series of loud farts could still be heard from within the Prime Minister's chambers.

"He will send for you," one of the guards politely echoed with an embarrassed curtsy.

The tiny, winged pair returned to the eline camp.

⸻ ◆ ⸻

"That didn't take very long," I queried, "How did it go?"

"We'll know tomorrow when the Prime Minister sends for us," Brendt answered with a roll of his eyes.

"Prime Minister, eh?" Cirdan snickered, "Where's Gig?"

"He stayed there," the Queen announced, "rest assured, we will be called on tomorrow."

"'Ow kin ye be so sure?" Balt inquired.

The Fairie Queen just smiled and winked, which apparently was a good enough answer for the dwarf.

Just at that moment, Captain Waxx and a large assembly of armed sailors arrived at the tent.

"Where be yor troops, Mon?" The captain asked with an almost disappointed look on his face.

Cirdan showed a fang filled smile and then roared long and loud.

Seconds later, a full unit of eline soldiers was attentively standing, armed and ready, just outside the door to the tent.

"Impressive," Byron commented.

The Scorpion's captain was awe struck.

The eline commander roared again, differently this time, ordering all but three soldiers clad in full black gear and black markings on lighter black coats, were dismissed.

The three remaining soldiers never moved a muscle, not even a twitch.

"Those three are here to train your men, Captain."

Byron and Balt both looked as though they'd just been granted a wish that they had been wishing for since childhood.

(For Balt, that was quite a long time ago!)

"Will my men be allowed to join in the training?" I asked and indicated the two fighters.

"You're all welcome to partake in the training," Cirdan granted.

I looked in Loher's direction to gauge her response to this news and she looked quite pleased...almost excited to learn new skills in the art of fighting.

"The sun has almost set," Cirdan announced, "get some rest, for tomorrow at sunup, we begin training!"

He gave out one last short roar and the three trainers finally snapped to life and returned to their tents.

Brendt and the fairies quietly disappeared in small groups and Captain Waxx dismissed his sailors.

They disembarked the tent area to return to The Scorpion, while my team gathered, this time around Balt and Byron, to convey their excitement for the next day's events.

I approached Cirdan as my team slowly, excitedly exited the tent, "I truly appreciate your willingness to train the men, I just wish that there was some way to give you the magical abilities that should rightfully and naturally be yours."

The eline commander just stood there, looking down at a map on the table, unblinking as if deep in thought.

I stood there for a moment, waiting for him to respond, but after a few minutes of silence, I began to turn to walk away.

I only had taken about three steps when he finally spoke, "Perhaps there is a way that we could acquire those abilities," he pondered.

I stopped, turned back around to face him and simply raised my right eyebrow.

He continued, "Your whole team, besides the dwarf and most of the adult humans all have magical abilities, correct?"

After a moment of serious thought, I agreed.

"Would it harm us to at least try to learn from you?" He rhetorically asked, "You could explain to us how you do what you do and perhaps we could tap into a part of us that we have never used before," he envisioned, becoming excited, "your red-haired human female, I believe she is called…Meeka; she had to learn magic, she wasn't born with it…"

His words had begun to make sense to me, and I found myself joining in his excitement, "I guess the worst that would happen is some time would be wasted," I agreed.

"But if we succeed," he breathed excitedly, "if we succeed... well then, my friend, then we would be unstoppable!"

It wasn't *what* he said, but it was *how he said it*, that sent a chill up my spine, made my skin crawl and made my heart jump all at once.

I was rapidly beginning to regret ever mentioning the word 'magic' and even putting any sort of idea into his head, as if I had just planted a poisonous seed to grow a race of twisted monsters.

I looked at him, attempted to fake a smile and slowly began to back away toward the door.

I had to get out of there, I had to distance myself from this situation for now and collect my wits as well as my thoughts.

Loher and Meeka would know what to do; they would make sense of this.

I casually hooked my thumb over my shoulder, back toward the door and feigned a laugh, "I should get back to my team," I excused, "it's been a long day, and I haven't eaten yet."

The fact that none of us had eaten yet finally dawned on him as well. "Bright and early tomorrow," he reminded with a cheesy wink, pointing a clawed finger at me as I backed out through the door.

I smiled and nodded and then turned around, headed with haste back to my camp.

My stomach was growling and felt extremely empty.

———◦———

Brother Fost was in fact, preparing a meal when I arrived at the camp.

I smiled at my fortune but then quickly remembered, I might have just spawned a race of monsters.

My mood fell low.

The last licks of sunlight were fading into the horizon, allowing the stars to have their time in the sky.

The fire was warm and inviting and the food Fost was cooking smelled delightful.

"What is that, Brother?" I asked, pointing to the meat over the flames.

"Which one?" The priest smiled, "There are three different types of meat here," he leaned in, closer to the fire and turned the first one, "this one is rabbit, the next is quail and last but not least, we have squirrel."

"It all be ta same ta me, Mate," Balt grunted from over the blade that he was sharpening.

"At least it's not fish again," Meeka quietly added.

"Yeah," Kuchoff agreed, "I'm so tired of fish."

"Where is everyone else?" I inquired.

"Loher is in your tent and Byron is over there, visiting with Mario," Meeka answered without even looking up from the...whatever it was that she was mending. I couldn't readily identify it.

"Mario, huh?" I teased.

"Well, that's his name, isn't it?" She asked, still consumed by the task at hand, "Mario Waxx?"

"Yes," I admitted quietly, "yes, I suppose it is."

I stood there for a moment, warming myself by the fire and then retreated to my tent.

Loher was inside, smoothing out the bedding that she had laid out for us to sleep in.

The flickering light from the fire made dancing shadows on the tent wall.

"Hello, stranger," she murmured as I ducked into the tent, "take off your boots before you come in here, I just cleaned up."

I stopped my foot mere centimeters from touching the blanket directly below it.

Loher smiled, "Sit down here," she patted the bedding next to her, "I'll help you take those off."

Somehow, I managed to maneuver myself from a standing position to my butt landing firmly on the extraordinarily soft bedding, all without letting my feet leave the outside of the tent.

"I'll just sit like this with my feet hanging out, for now." I decided.

"Why?" She asked.

"I'll just have to put them back on in order to go eat," I explained. "Besides, there is something that I need to discuss with you and Mee-ka."

Loher giggled and then asked, "What do you want to discuss with us?"

I took a deep breath and began, "I think I might have created some sort of monster in Cirdan."

"How so?"

"It has to do with arcane magic," I disclosed, "I really think Meeka should be involved."

Loher sat up and crawled to the tent opening, stuck her head out and got Meeka's attention.

"You called?" Meeka asked as she arrived at our tent a moment later.

"Come on in, Meeka," I coaxed, "I think there may be a problem that you might be able to help me with."

"It involves your type of magic," Loher explained.

Meeka slipped off her boots and came inside; Loher shot me a look of 'see? She didn't even have to be asked to take her boots off.'

I find it amazing that one simple look from a woman can relay so much information... if you're paying attention.

The only problem with that is, most men don't know how to decipher said information and are brutally condemned for it.

"Magic is my specialty," Meeka giggled.

"The floor is yours, Thunor." Loher offered.

"Yes," I admitted, "I understand that she took her boots off before she came in without being asked to do so," I blurted without thinking.

"Well, it's just common practice to..." Meeka began until I cut her off...

... Still toward Loher and a bit heated, "Your attitude was all jokey, lovey dovey even after you 'had to ask' me to take my boots off, until she comes in and automatically does it, and now I'm in trouble?"

"No, My Love," Loher corrected calmly, with a slight giggle, "my attitude changed as soon as you admitted that this magic problem is probably your fault."

"Ta plot thickens!" Balt snorted jovially from outside.

"BALT!" The three of us barked in unison.

"Wot?"

"Would somebody please explain to me what's going on?" Meeka cried in confusion.

By now, the whole team was gathered by the mouth of my tent, "Everybody comfy? Good." I started.

Without going into great detail, but still reporting enough, I explained how the eline are upset that they are half elven and have no magical abilities, while I'm also half elven and I do have magical abilities.

To make matters worse, they believe that Kuchoff is my son, which would make him one quarter elven and even he has magical abilities, better than my own, I reluctantly added.

With this information, false as some of it is, one can only imagine how jealous and angry the eline probably are at this point in the game.

So, in order to keep the peace between our two parties, I expressed how I wished that there was a way to give them the magic that naturally should be theirs and that Cirdan came up with the idea that perhaps we, specifically Meeka, could teach them how to use magic.

"I don't see a problem with that," Meeka offered, and Loher agreed.

"With magical abilities," I began slowly to gain everyone's attention, "can you even conceive how powerful and unstoppable they would become?"

I gave everyone a few seconds to ponder that thought before I completed with...

... "They do," I stated. "They realize that with magic, they will be virtually unstoppable. Cirdan brought it to my attention, and I didn't like how he said it."

One by one, all but Balt, the look of terror slowly washed over my companion's faces.

"Oh no!" Brother Fost exclaimed.

"What is it?" Loher asked, surprised.

"I almost forgot about dinner!" The halfling cried and bounded off to the fire as fast as his little legs could carry him.

I have never, in the whole time that I have known him, seen him move so quickly, not even in battle.

"It's okay," he called, "I saved it!"

"It's not burned?" Byron asked as he approached the fire.

"No," the halfling answered, "but it's done, let's eat."

Meeka slipped her boots back on and shot a fake menacing look at me before she left the tent.

Loher leaned over and quickly kissed me and then grabbed my hands to pull me up and out of the tent with her.

Hand in hand, Loher and I followed the wizard to the fire and joined our friends in the meal.

While we ate, we quietly discussed our problem and it was decided that it wasn't directly my fault, this was bound to happen one way or another, but now we somehow had to fix it...soon.

We retired to our tents before we could come to a solution to the magical problem.

It had just gotten too late, and our minds weren't working so well, so we decided to call it a night and discuss it in the morning before we headed to the training.

Most of us were asleep when Captain Waxx quietly woke me up.

I opened my eyes and saw Loher and the captain standing above me with concern written on their faces, "What's wrong?" I asked, trying to keep my eyes open.

"There's a few ships heading toward The Scorpion, and they don't look friendly," Loher whispered.

"How does a ship look unfriendly?" I asked, eyes open but still half asleep.

"When it be soundin' like it be fulla raiders an' marauders an' shootin' arrows at'cha, Mon, dat be when it look unfriendly."

Now, fully awake, I jumped up and pulled my boots on, "It's that close?"

"Aye."

"Do you think we should get the eline involved?" Loher asked as she headed to Meeka's tent.

"I'm sure they're aware of it by now," I called back, "with all of the noise we're making."

I checked Balt and Byron's tent and found it empty and before I could ask where they were, I caught a glimpse of Balt and his Great Axe standing near the shoreline shouting obscenities at the oncoming ships.

He asked for a battle; he's about to get one.

CHAPTER SIX

CONSILIUM

My team and I stood there on the beach with our weapons ready for battle, watching the enemy ships slowly approach.

Our nerves, however, were not ready.

I looked down at my feet and noticed a rat.

For every enemy arrow that came within a meter of our group, Meeka would lob a magical ball of fire in the general direction of the oncoming ships.

"Yer aim canna be tat bad, Meeka," Balt grunted.

Meeka laughed, "No, Balt, I'm just playing with them; if I really wanted to hit them, I would."

"Prove it, Lass." Balt dared the wizard, "b'sides, why ain't ye tryin' te kill 'em?"

Meeka smiled and drew her hand back as if she was about to throw a stone into the water, but when she threw her hand forward, instead of a stone, a magical ball of flame was launched from the palm of her hand and screamed through the air toward the approaching ship, "Because this is too easy. A girl likes a challenge occasionally."

With deadly accuracy, the fireball exploded against the bow of the closest ship, engulfing everything from the bow to the foremast.

Flames danced across the forecastle deck and climbed the foremast, consuming the jibs, the fore staysail and the foresail.

Thick smoke belched into the air, muting the dimmer stars while the ship began to veer off course.

Pieces of flaming sail began to descend to the deck below, causing even more destruction.

The flames must have ignited a powder keg or two, because after what only seemed like a short moment, the whole enemy ship exploded with a quick bright flash followed by an equally loud bang.

Chunks of flaming wood exploded into the night sky and lit up the area enough for us to see a large group of orc and hobgoblin raiders swimming to shore.

Flaming shrapnel impacted the other ships, so they spread out in case of another explosion.

Meeka gasped in horror and amazement, "That was a lucky shot," she admitted.

"Yer too modest," Balt chuckled in fascination.

Silent movement behind us reported an equally large group of eline soldiers quickly making their way to the beach.

"We've got company," Byron and I said at the same time.

Loher tossed Kuchoff one of her bows and the pair quickly began picking off swimming raiders, and as the enemy ships began to sink, more and more of them began to swim ashore in smaller groups.

By the time the first wave of raiders reached us, so did the mob of eline.

The sounds of war rang out into the night and although the enemy outnumbered us approximately twelve to one, their numbers began to dwindle as these creatures had apparently never encountered eline before and were caught completely unprepared.

My infrared vision was virtually useless due to the thick black smoke and the random flashes from Meeka's fireballs; it was difficult to determine friend from foe.

The only light we had was the flickering flames of the rapidly sinking ship and the smoldering corpses from the occasional fireball that Meeka conjured with deadly accuracy.

Staying on my feet had become increasingly difficult as well, due to the ever-growing blanket of bodies that littered the ground beneath our feet.

The stench of burning flesh overpowered my senses, adding to the difficulty and danger.

I was becoming distracted by my own thoughts of the safety of my team, and I feared that if I was having so much difficulty in this fight, why wouldn't the rest of my team?

An arrow suddenly whizzed past my ear and impacted into the soft, moist flesh of someone, or something, directly behind me and I heard the distinct sound of a moan as the air was forced out of the victim's lungs as it crumpled to the ground, dead.

My intuition told me to raise my sword up to protect my face, so I instantly did and blocked a blade from slicing my head in two.

Suddenly, as I attempted to take a step forward, I tripped over a body and went down to my hands and knees.

Without thinking, I felt around to determine what or who it was that I had tripped over...

All I felt was fur.

Blood-soaked fur.

Next to the eline body, I found a dagger, short and extremely light for its size.

I decided to wield this dagger in my left hand while continuing with my own sword in my right.

The sun had finally begun to peak over the horizon, providing welcome light.

I could almost see now, making out faint shapes and movement through the thick, dark smoke.

A large creature loomed ahead of me, but I didn't attack until I saw the unmistakable shape of orc tusks.

It was charging toward me, slowing down just enough to gain the proper footing to swing its blade at me.

I blocked the attack with my left blade and counter attacked with my right.

Amazingly, my left blade deflected the orc blade with little to no recoil and seemed to actually absorb the impact and transfer the energy into my right blade as it effortlessly sliced through not only the orc's thick leather armor, but also through its shoulder down into the bone.

My blade easily slid out of the wound as the orc fell to the ground clutching its shoulder.

Without thinking, I plunged my new eline blade and extinguished the orc's life flame.

It seemed as if the dagger acted all on its own.

I quickly took advantage of the increasing light and looked around to see if I could catch a glimpse of any of my team but there were too many eline, hobgoblins and orcs in the way, not to mention another three orcs attempting to blitz attack me.

Miraculously, accurately aimed arrows from what I assumed was a friendly bow, defeated two of the three beasts, leaving the odds in my favor as the surviving orc was suddenly surprised and confused at the abrupt deaths of his comrades.

My right blade found purchase in the oncoming orc's ribcage while the blade of a familiar battle axe cleaved its skull in half from behind.

"Was tat me kill er yers?" Balt asked as he wiped the dead orc's blood from his face.

"You can have it," I breathed as I lunged over the smiling dwarf's shoulder and slit the throat of yet another orc raider, "because that one's mine."

"Bravo," the dwarven warrior laughed and disappeared into the carnage.

As my gaze followed my friend into the crowd, I witnessed another few raiders discover their deaths due to a nasty case of arrows to the head.

As Balt disappeared into the carnage, I caught a quick glimpse of Byron cutting down a large hobgoblin and then also disappearing into the fray.

My attention was suddenly focused on a slim, shadow-black eline, wielding two swords, flipping high into the air above a pair of confused orcs.

Her blades found success, slicing through each of their necks as she swiftly landed behind her opponents; their heads landing neatly in the laps of their respective owners.

It was pure artwork.

I suddenly found myself surrounded by a mixed group of mostly orcs and a few hobgoblins.

My heart began to beat a bit more rapidly from the anxiety of being surrounded by so many foes.

I quickly looked around in hopes of locating a friendly face but found no one.

I was alone; it was completely up to me.

My heart began to beat faster.

The first hit was from a dull blade that just deflected off the chest plate I was still wearing under my tunic.

The impact caused me to lose my footing, and I went down on one knee.

Rats were already munching on the dead, there were hundreds of them.

The second hit came from behind from some sort of blunt weapon or perhaps a foot or fist; the impact severely weakened my stance, and I ended up virtually face down in the middle of a puddle of blood and gore.

Rats scattered as my face splashed into the mud.

Rudely, one of my attackers decided to step on the back of my head, mashing my face into the blood-soaked ground.

This was his fatal mistake...

... Mud (and blood) began to fill my mouth and nose, and the taste must have triggered some latent abilities left over from being undead.

I began to push myself up and out from under whoever or whatever was standing on me as I felt my body gather renewed supernatural strength.

I grabbed the foot and ankle of my oppressor and twisted it.

The weight was reduced as the creature unsteadily toppled from my back, and I effortlessly stood up, still grasping the leg of the now frightened ogre three times my size.

I slowly pulled the ogre closer with his leg as it struggled against my regained superior strength.

It slashed at me with its sword, but to no avail.

As I pulled, it got snagged on a rock or root, so, I tugged as hard as I could, and pulled its leg right out of the socket.

I then proceeded to beat it in the face with its own leg until its head caved in.

I tossed the leg aside, and continued to look for what I now considered, *victims*.

A blanket of rats had gathered at my feet.

Shortly, another orc was attempting to hack at me with a crude blade.

The blade sliced neatly into my hip, and I could feel its impact stop on my bone, yet I didn't immediately react.

I just stood there, looking into its eyes.

I'd like to tell you that these creatures are unthinking, unfeeling and brainless, but that would be incorrect.

This orc *knew* it was in trouble and it was definitely *feeling* fear as I slowly reached out and grasped it by the throat.

I picked the creature up by the throat, lifting it a few inches off the ground as my fingers began to tighten and squeeze.

The orc dropped its weapon and began to claw at my hand around its neck, struggling for air as it slowly passed out.

I felt its esophagus collapse in my hand as the life force escaped into the aether.

The body went limp, so I let my grasp go and the corpse crumbled to the ground in a heap by my feet.

Rats immediately covered the corpse.

I heard another explosion as the final ship became a blazing inferno and then slowly sunk into the sea.

More hobgoblins and orcs were swimming to shore, and I noticed a long line of sailors and eline warriors, standing at the water's edge, waiting for the next phase of battle.

I strode toward the sea, stepping over the bodies of orcs, hobgoblins, eline and unfortunately, a few humans.

The aroma of blood and smoke filled the air as a dying hobgoblin reached out and grabbed for my leg.

I felt the eline dagger I had picked up begin to vibrate on my belt, as I unsheathed it without thinking and involuntarily plunged the blade into the hobgoblin's brain and put it out of its misery.

My face suddenly began to itch, so I wiped the already drying blood and debris from my face and continued to search for my friends as I made my way to the water's edge.

The smoke was thick in the air, making it nearly impossible to breathe and even more difficult to see more than a meter in front of your own face.

I could feel my vampiric strength begin to slowly fade and I started feeling more and more like myself again.

I looked down and the rats were all but gone.

The final few raiders were being finished off as I arrived at the water's edge.

A collective roar of victory ensued as the sounds of battle began to fade away and I realized that we had won.

Had it not been for the eline defenders coming to our aid, my team and I, including the captain and crew of The Scorpion, would have probably been lost.

My team slowly began to regroup among the carnage strewn over the beach and as I made my way to the group, I found Kuchoff, crying over the barely recognizable corpse of our very own Byron Le'Abboltt.

My heart sank as a lump began to grow in my throat and tears welled up in my eyes.

I stood there in disbelief and slight horror, staring at my dead friend.

Kuchoff looked up with tears in his eyes as he noticed me standing there.

He slowly stood up and began to walk toward me, stopping only to retrieve the Shino Sutoka Katana; the legendary weapon was safe.

Not only did we have something to remember our friend by, but we also possessed one of the most recognizable, trusted and respected (or feared) weapons ever known to the mortal (and immortal) world.

He secured the weapon to his back, and we began to walk back toward our friends.

As we approached, it was painfully obvious that everyone understood what had happened, yet no words were ever spoken about it.

Instead, we spoke of the battle, we spoke of glory, we spoke of honor, and we spoke of the eline.

The group of surviving eline began to make their way as a group, led by a large tiger striped male, toward us.

"Your training is complete," the leader announced, "those of you that survived require no more training; you act as a team in a most efficient manner."

"By whose authority do you speak?" Brother Fost boldly and uncharacteristically spoke.

"By my authority," Cirdan announced as he appeared from behind a dune, "you fought well."

"All but one of you," the large tiger striped eline chuckled, "I'm highly surprised that young man is still alive," he said, pointing at Kuchoff.

With absolutely no warning, Kuchoff clapped his hands and silently screamed something inaudible, probably in an archaic language, and suddenly the large tiger striped eline dropped to the sand and began to writhe around in pain.

Cirdan's eyes went wide, and he took a dozen steps away from his soldier.

Meeka put her hands over her open mouth and gasped in horror.

Kuchoff slowly walked toward the struggling eline and upon reaching him, bent over and took his victim's face in his hands, "I could kill you just by thinking about it," he warned through gritted teeth and then released the creature and looked up at the crowd, "I suggest that you all remember that."

There was silence as the eline regained his composure, slowly stood back up and brushed the sand out of his fur.

Kuchoff slowly backed away for a few steps, turned around and walked back to where he was standing next to Meeka, who was considerably shaken by what she had just witnessed.

I must admit that I too, was somewhat shocked at the apparent ease with which he dropped a creature that was twice his size.

"Apparently, we have proven ourselves to you in battle," I announced, "now you must prove yourselves to us."

"What do we need to prove to you?" Cirdan asked, obviously shaken as well, still staring at Kuchoff.

Before I could speak, Meeka spoke up, "You must prove to us that you're worthy of the magical training that you've all but demanded from us."

Cirdan nodded and looked down at his feet, almost as if in defeat.

With that, we took our leave and bid the eline a good day.

We waded once again, through the sea of blood and corpses, and began to walk back to our encampment.

Something seemed off.

Meeka was uncharacteristically quiet.

As soon as we entered the clearing, Meeka suddenly stopped and faced Kuchoff.

"Explain, young man," Meeka sternly coughed at Kuchoff, stepping on her tiptoes to be eye to eye with him, gripping him tightly by the shoulders.

She looked angry and scared all at once.

Kuchoff had a genuine look of surprise on his face and was completely unprepared for Meeka's sudden parental outburst, "We needed to maintain control in our favor," he began, shaky at first, but calmly and confidently continued, "I think I might have just secured it indefinitely."

Meeka loosened her grip on his shoulders and looked him in the eyes, "Can you really do what you said in there?"

Kuchoff smiled his usual toothy grin, "No," he blinked, "but I sure convinced everyone that I could, and that's all that matters."

Meeka breathed a sigh of relief and let go of his shoulders.

He smiled and tussled Meeka's hair as we began to walk back to our encampment.

"We only knew him for a short time, but we learned to love and trust this man we now lay to rest," Kuchoff choked through the obvious lump in his throat.

Or perhaps it was his voice beginning to change from boy to man?

"Byron Le'Abboltt." The rest of us chanted in unison as the boy placed the final stone on the burial cairn.

After a moment of silence, we gathered and began walking back to the cove.

"That was such a lovely place for a funeral," Meeka softly voiced.

"Did you notice all of the butterflies?" Brother Fost replied half excitedly.

"It seemed as though there were clouds of them at times!" Loher blurted in disbelief.

"That big one..." Kuchoff smiled.

We all turned and looked at him.

"Did you see the big one?" He asked in bewilderment, "That big, beautiful butterfly?"

We all shook our heads and continued walking.

"Where did you see it?" Meeka asked after a moment.

"When I was on top of the mound, placing the last stone, I looked at you and it was hovering right behind Thunor's head." He answered, apparently pointing at me.

I felt very small as I realized that all eyes were suddenly on the back of my head.

I stopped in my tracks and slowly turned around as everyone slowed to a stop.

"Behind, my head?" I asked. "Well, then Loher, you should have seen it, you were standing right next to me." I chuckled.

"Sorry, I didn't see it," she admitted, "I was too distracted by Balt's incessant chanting."

"Incessant?" Balt spat, obviously offended, "Ye ave yer traditions, we ave ours."

"He wasn't a dwarf, Balt." Brother Fost explained.

"I think what he means," I cut in before Balt could react, "is that Byron was a brother warrior, and Balt was only respecting warrior traditions."

"Aye," Balt agreed, whether I was correct or to end the discussion and draw the attention away from him, I'm not completely sure.

"She's my sister." A disembodied voice announced as butterflies and fairies began to appear as if from thin air.

"Why must ye always perch on me helmet?" Balt roared, drawing everyone's attention to him once again.

"It makes such a nice stage, Dear." The Fairie Queen answered in a matter of a fact tone and forcibly tapped the end of her staff on the top of Balt's helm, creating a bit of a bell tone.

Balt growled and reluctantly allowed the intrusion into his personal bubble.

"Yer lucky yer all so tiny," the dwarf grumbled and shifted his weight from one foot to the other.

Standing with her was none other than the big, beautiful butterfly that was allegedly hovering behind my head at the funeral, only this wasn't a butterfly at all...

⸻ ◆ ⸻

"Who are you?" Loher asked in awe, apparently unable, or unwilling to suppress her fascination.

The 'butterfly creature' gracefully took to the air and gently landed on Loher's outstretched hand. "I am the Butterfly Queen," she announced.

We all looked toward the Fairie Queen for clarification.

The Fairie Queen smiled and laughed, "We were born into a large family that was handpicked eons ago by the ancient elders of our elders." The Fairie Queen began, "Of the six children in our immediate family, four of us were girls, the other two, were boys.

The boys were almost sent away, like all boys are in every family, to train and become soldiers or hunters or whatever else boys do, but because of the nobility of our family, our brothers were kept at home.

My three sisters and I were prepped and trained to become Queens; I am the Queen of the more commonly known fairies; The Dragonfly sect.

My sister here is the Queen of the Butterfly sect.

Our other two sisters are the Queens of the Beetle sect and the Bee sect."

"The Butterfly Queen continued, "Our brothers became the kings of their own sects, the Spiders, and the Ants."

"Is there a Dragonfly King?" I asked.

"Yes," the Butterfly Queen answered, although I was expecting the Dragonfly Queen to answer, "My husband is the Dragonfly King."

"Wot?" Balt croaked, "But..." he stammered in confusion, pointing to the top of his helmet and then pointing at Loher's hand and then back again.

"So, are you married to the Butterfly King?" I asked.

The Dragonfly Queen laughed, "No, the Bee Queen is married to the Butterfly King.

I, nor the Beetle Queen, are married." She paused, "Interested?" She teased with a wink to Loher.

Loher smiled and nudged me closer to the Dragonfly Queen.

"Well, it's about time for my sister and me to continue our meeting with the Prime Minister of Errfordland." The Dragonfly Queen announced with a smile.

The Royal pair gingerly took flight and mixed in with the rest of the fae-folk and then gradually disappeared.

———— ◆ ————

"McLaaud," a pirate called as we returned to the cove, "You have to come see this."

"Where's Captain Waxx?" I asked.

"Aboard the enemy's wreckage," he answered, "the captain, he found something."

"Show me." As I took off into a jog along with the pirate.

The pirate began running towards a small dingy tied to some driftwood right on the water's edge.

When we got there, we both climbed in and shoved off.

By the time the pirate and I arrived at the wreckage, a large plume of pink smoke was dissipating to reveal the rest of my team standing aboard the wreckage, all with goofy smiles on their faces.

"What took you so long?" Meeka teased as she grabbed my wrist to help me over the railing.

I just smiled and shook my head as I allowed her to guide me over the railing and onto the wrecked enemy ship.

I turned to gauge the pirate's reaction to the situation and found that he too was actually laughing.

It seemed as though the pirates had gotten used to Meeka's mystics.

Suddenly, we heard several large splashes directly near the opposite side of the ship.

We all started running toward the sounds to investigate; as we came around to get a better look, we witnessed several pirates dumping orc corpses over the railing and into the sea.

"It keeps the sharks over here and away from where we bathe and hunt." The pirate explained, "Come, the captain wants to show you something."

"Please tell me that you searched those bodies before you dumped them over," Loher pled.

"Aye, Ma'am," the pirate smiled, "there's a pile of effects down below, come, I'll show you."

He led us to the stairs leading below decks and told us to be careful on the way down and then disappeared into the darkness below.

The stairs were broken and splintering but the captain must have ordered someone to affix a shoddy rope ladder to take their place.

"Follow my lead and do exactly what I do." Loher offered as she exaggerated her moves in order to emphasize the correct places to step and hold on to.

As soon as she reached the bottom, she turned around to see the rest of us standing there with goofy grins on our faces, surrounded by Meeka's pink smoke.

"Vera graceful," Balt teased.

Loher smiled and lightly punched him in the shoulder.

"Mr. McLaaud," Captain Waxx greeted, "We tink we intercepted a message, Mon. Maybe intended for our muscle-bound fur friends."

"Why do you think that?" I asked, intrigued.

The pirate captain only grinned and hooked his thumb over his shoulder, pointing to a large blood stain on the wall and floor.

I faintly heard Balt chuckle.

Gems, coins, and other interesting trinkets were piled up in the corner.

Loher took immediate interest.

"D'ere was also dis," he said as he handed Brother Fost a rolled-up letter, "we tried to decipher it, but..." He frowned, then bowed and gracefully turned away.

"Hmm..." the halfling priest murmured as he studied the parchment, "this is written in Old Elven," he paused, "only not written by elven hands." The priest examined.

"Can you tell who, or what wrote it?" I asked.

"Someone with meaty hands, like an orc," Brother Fost paused in thought, "or a dwarf..."

"Oi, now," Balt growled.

"...Or a large human could have written it." The priest hastily added.

"Hey, Meeka," Loher called from behind the large pile of baubles, "take a look at this!"

Meeka quickly strode over to where Loher was crouching and looked behind the pile, "Well, hello there," Meeka exclaimed, "What's your name?"

This got everybody's attention.

Meeka leaned over and retrieved whatever it was off the floor.

Still partially hidden behind the pile, it looked as though she was petting something.

"You're so beautiful," she cooed, "I think I'm going to keep you!"

"Are you sure it's not dangerous?" Loher asked.

"I'll have to keep an eye on it until I know it better, but for now," the wizard turned and faced everyone, "I'm sure we'll all be just fine."

In her hands, she held out a jewel encrusted glass and crystal wand.

"I think I just translated this scroll." Brother Fost announced, unintentionally interrupting Meeka and Loher's display.

"Can you read it to me?" I prompted.

"It's going to be a rough translation, but the main information is..." the priest took a deep breath and began, "...The Grand Ascendancy has no idea where we, The Scorpion specifically, are, they sent these ships to inform the eline of our existence and to treat us like a threat."

"Dey must've been surprised ta see De Scorpion already sittin' 'ere when dey arrived, Mon." Captain Waxx laughed.

"S'prize!" Balt roared in laughter, splaying his fingers out like a fan fair.

"Well, it's a good thing we intercepted this message," I stated, calming the room, "but the Grand Ascendancy will surely be expecting their ships back soon and when they don't show up, they might send another ship out looking for it."

"Do we tell the eline about this?" Brother Fost asked.

"No!" I quickly decided, "I have an odd feeling that we can trust them, but only as long as they never view us as a threat, not even a small threat."

"Should we still train them in magic?" Meeka asked, still admiring the wand Loher had found for her.

After a moment's thought I answered, "Yes, but keep it basic for now, like light spells and healing until we know if we can trust them or not."

"I vote we get most of our stuff back aboard The Scorpion in case we have to leave in a hurry," Kuchoff blurted.

Shocked and impressed that the youngster had finally spoken up with a suggestion, we all just stared at him.

"Ta boy-o gots a guid point." Balt admitted after a thoughtful moment.

"If the eline see that we're packing up," I began, "they'll probably become suspicious and come snooping around."

"Meeka and I will keep them distracted with the magical training Cirdan so desperately wants," Loher offered, slugging Meeka on the shoulder.

Kuchoff snapped his fingers and smiled, "We could just leave enough of a camp left over to make it look like we have no intentions of leaving, while all of the important stuff is actually safe aboard the ship."

We discussed plans for the immediate future for the rest of the evening until one by one, our party members became too tired to think and retired for the night.

The next morning, while the pirates and a few of my companions began to load up the ship, Meeka, Kuchoff, Loher and I decided to visit Cirdan and his troops to offer the magical training they wanted as well as to keep most of them occupied while the storage transfer took place.

We found Cirdan and a few of his top trusted men having breakfast in the map tent.

Cirdan turned with a smile and began to welcome us into the tent until he saw Kuchoff.

His welcoming smile suddenly disappeared and the eline warrior's casual demeanor quickly turned cold.

"May I offer you something to eat?" Cirdan offered, ushering all non-essential personnel out of the tent, "Something to drink?"

His reaction to Kuchoff was completely unexpected and made me feel a little uneasy, until I realized if I or one of my companions had been the subject of Kuchoff's power like Cirdan witnessed, I think my attitude toward Kuchoff would be similar.

A few of us accepted some breakfast and we sat down to eat.

"We thought we would stop by and see if you were ready for that magical training you wanted." Meeka conversed between bites of food.

I looked up from my plate and noticed that Cirdan and a few of his men were focused on Kuchoff as if he was about to perform some sort of trick or extraordinary feat; the eline soldier did not reply.

"Are you ready for the training?" she asked after a moment.

Several minutes passed as the catlike soldiers continued their gaze.

"My mom asked you a question." Kuchoff calmly stated.

Cirdan snapped out of his state of being and answered, "Wh-? The training?" He blinked, "Yes, yes, the training. My men and I discussed the training in length and have agreed to forgo the magical training."

A wave of confusion filled the tent.

Recognizing the confused looks on our faces, Cirdan explained, "We decided that your son is powerful enough that we won't need the training and that if we all live through the upcoming battle, we shall return to Beornan Heafod with you and live out the remainder of our years among our blood cousins, the elves."

"We won't have any reason to stay here if The Grand Ascendancy is destroyed," one of Cirdan's men added.

"That will have to be discussed with the elven elders," an unfamiliar female voice announced as the outside of the tent began to become covered in butterflies.

"We're under attack!" an eline soldier shouted as he burst into the tent waving his arms around in a flurry; hundreds of butterflies followed in after.

"Stand down," Cirdan ordered, "Tell all of the men to stand down."

Kuchoff began to giggle, making Meeka and I softly giggle, as the soldier exited the tent shouting commands here and there as butterflies feigned failed, feeble attempts at their lives.

"Where's my stage?" The Butterfly Queen asked with a pout as she looked around for Balt.

"Balt didn't come with us, Your Majesty," I called and stretched out my hand for her to land on.

Instead, she decided to perch upon Kuchoff's head with a gentle landing, "My sister, the Dragonfly Queen, also known as the Fairie Queen, is just finishing up with the meeting between Prime Minister Pik of the Errfords and I can tell you that it looks promising."

Meeka and Kuchoff shot toothy smiles at each other at the sound of the good news.

"However," she announced, "there may be some potentially bad news, but I'll wait for her to tell you that, as it may not be true."

"What does it have to do with?" I asked.

"The cooperation of all parties involved." She vaguely answered.

CHAPTER SEVEN

DE PERQUISITIONE

P rime Minister Pik settled into the makeshift yet comfortable chair that Balt had thrown together just before the meeting was called to order.

His girth oozed over the sides of the chair in a most foul manner.

"I knew I shulda made it bigger," Balt cursed under his breath, "but I'm gonna laugh if it falls apart."

The Butterfly Queen, Dragonfly Queen and Brendt settled together on top of Balt's helm, as Balt himself sat lazily in a chair at the end of the table and stared off into space listening for the key words, 'Fight', 'Battle' and 'Kill' along with any other terms of destruction.

Brother Fost sat across from the dwarf, prepared to take notes in case anyone became lost or confused.

At the opposite end of the table sat Cirdan and two of his most trusted eline soldiers, as Loher and I sat directly across from them.

The rest of my team sat randomly about the table attempting to understand the terms and conditions in which the errfords would agree to help us.

Dozens of fairies and butterflies were perched around the tent in various locations while several other errfords scurried around silently, trying to find the best spots to see and hear from, yet actively maintaining a safe distance from the eline.

"Before this meeting goes into anything too far," Pik began, "I want it to be clear that we are not going to help anyone as long as those eline are involved."

"Awwe," Balt chuckled under his breath, "shut down b'fore it even b'gan."

"We came to this meeting..." Cirdan replied, "no, we hosted this meeting to show good faith that we have stopped hunting you."

"Only because you have not been successful in killing any of us," Pik countered, side-eyeing the eline commander.

"They're no longer a threat to you." I calmly vouched.

"I'm not even sure we can trust you!" The Prime Minister spat, pointing at me, drool oozing down his chins.

"Then why are you here, Prime Minister?" The Fairie Queen sternly asked.

The portly errford attempted to dramatically stand up quickly but failed and only proceeded to ooze into a slightly less comfortable looking position than before, "I want you all off of my island," he gurgled from under his own weight, "We just want to be left in peace."

Cirdan suddenly rose from his chair and snatched the Prime Minister from his seat and then gently replaced him back, into a more comfortable position.

"I could have killed you just now," the eline leader cooed as he gently brushed a few crumbs and dust from the Prime Minister's coat and then returned back to his own chair, "but instead, I decided to help you."

As if a delayed reaction, a light blue orb of light suddenly surrounded Pik's body and scorched some of the loose bark from the sticks used to make up his chair.

Balt's attention was piqued.

Embarrassed, Pik attempted to hide his face behind a fold in the loose robes he wore and then decided his tail would do the trick.

"This is ridiculous," Brendt stammered as he took flight and hovered over the center of the table. "When I first met this group of strangers, I was convinced that they were hunting me..."

"We were," Balt breathed quietly with a wry smile.

"You're a stranger to us as well," Pik snorted, peeking from behind his bushy tail, and then turned toward Cirdan, "You're right," he said, finally showing his face, "You could have killed me just now, but I'm still not completely convinced that your intentions are real... None of you."

I leaned across the table and told Cirdan, just loud enough for Pik to hear, "That was a foolish thing to do. We've seen what the errfords are capable of."

Realizing I was trying to boost Pik's confidence and attempt to inflate the Prime Minister's ego, the eline leader nodded in agreement and feigned a self-ashamed look.

The Errford Prime Minister fell for our charade, puffed out his oversized chest, cleared his throat and asked in a bold voice, "What exactly are we dealing with? How and why are you 'stuck' on my island and would someone please tell me what The Grand Ascendancy is?"

The Fairie Queen rolled her eyes and planted her hand firmly upon her own face, shaking her head.

Before anyone else could speak, an eline soldier suddenly poked his head into the tent and announced, "Sir, our sentries have spotted several ships on the horizon headed in this direction."

"Define, 'several' ships," Pik asked, assuming 'Sir' meant 'Pik' and not 'Cirdan.'

The soldier shot Cirdan a confused look.

"Answer the Prime Minister," Cirdan ordered with an amused smile.

"Twenty ships?" The soldier both asked and answered in confusion as he alternated his attention between his commander and the Prime Minister.

"Very well," Pik replied and dismissed the soldier with a rude wave, "that will be all."

Cirdan smiled and nodded, allowing the soldier to leave.

"D'ja hear tat?" Balt smiled, "Twenty ships full o' ta enemy. Hedded tis way." The dwarf hopped off of his chair sending the three fae folk fluttering for somewhere to land and proceeded toward the exit, Great Axe in hand.

"The enemy?" Pik asked, suddenly nervous again.

"The Grand Ascendancy," I answered as I too got up from my seat and headed for the door.

⋅◆⋅

"Captain Waxx!" I called as we arrived at the cove, "Get The Scorpion ready!"

"Ready fer wot, Mon?" The captain asked as he tried to calm me down from my run.

Doubled over, out of breath and panting, I raised my left arm and hand into a pointing position and simply pointed to the horizon.

That picture was worth more than a thousand words, as was the look on the captain's face when he finally saw our approaching opponents.

Without a word, Captain Waxx snapped into action and raced aboard The Scorpion.

Moments later (sooner than I thought it would take), The Scorpion was headed out to sea...

...Without me or anyone from my team.

"They're leaving without us!" Loher yelled as she ran up to me.

"Where's Balt?" I asked, worried he might be aboard.

"Balt?" She questioned, "They're leaving without us!" She snapped, pointing at The Scorpion.

"Yes, where is he?" I asked, steadying her by her shoulders and making her focus on me, "Was Balt aboard that ship?"

Loher blinked a few times and focused, "Balt? I don't know. Why?"

"Oi! [something inaudible], I'm right 'ere, Mate, but where ta [something inaudible] are tey goin'?" The dwarf cursed as soon as he was close enough to us to hear.

"He's right there," Loher said and jabbed a finger into my side.

"Tey're leavin' witout us," Balt sadly echoed.

"What happened in the meeting?" Brother Fost asked from behind me as if he just appeared from out of thin air.

I quickly turned around, slightly startled by the unexpected sound of his voice.

He stood there, looking like he was ready for anything; a determined look on his face and his Blessed Crossbow in his hands, "I saw everyone rush out of the tent," he explained, "You were screaming something about getting the ship ready, so I grabbed my gear and came back, but by the time I returned..." He finished by gesturing toward The Scorpion.

"Where are Meeka and Kuchoff?" Loher suddenly asked.

"I passed their tent on my way back," the priest replied, "it didn't look like they were there, but I can't be sure."

"Go back and see if they're there or on their way back yet," I suggested to Brother Fost, "I'm going to go back to the eline camp and see if they went that way."

"What do you want us to do?" Loher asked.

"One of you, go with Fost and one of you, with me."

"Well," Balt laughed, "Ta choice be obvious Lass."

Loher just shot him a playful sneer and grabbed my arm.

I could still hear Balt's laughter as Loher and I began to run back to the camp.

***

As we reached the compound with all of the eline tents, we noticed that the soldiers, although battle ready, were not gathering in their squads in preparation for the upcoming battle.

"Something seems a little weird to me here," Loher stated.

"Agreed," I commented, "Shouldn't they be—"

"Marching to the cove?" Cirdan asked as he appeared in the opening to his tent.

Loher and I just stood there in silence.

"Don't worry," Cirdan continued, "We will be there when we're needed. The ships are still far out to sea." He swept his clawed hand toward the horizon, "We have plenty of time."

"Have you seen Meeka?" Loher asked, "Or Kuchoff?"

"Not since everyone ran out of here at the news of the advancing ships." Cirdan replied and tightened the shoulder strap on his armor.

Suddenly, we began to hear cannon fire off in the distance.

Looking out to the sea, I could see faint flashes of light between The Scorpion and the next closest ship.

The flashes of light were soon followed by low banging sounds.

Balt and Brother Fost could also be seen as they wound their way through a clearing in the tall grasses that led to this camp; they were alone.

Everyone's attention was suddenly turned toward the sea as one of the enemy ships rapidly sank below the surface of the water and disappeared.

"Atta-boy-o, Waxxy!" Balt spewed without trying to hold in his pride.

"They're still too far out to sea to successfully swim to shore," Cirdan offered and then echoed, "We still have time."

"So, we're just going to stand here and wait?" Our priest asked.

"I know it's not something that you want to hear, Brother Fost," Loher began, "but, yes."

"E wouldn't-a asked if e' didn't wanna know, Lass."

"Would you two please stop your bickering back and forth?" Brendt asked, literally appearing from out of thin air. "You both are part of a team!" The sprite added, "The same team."

Loher began to laugh.

Brendt looked confused.

Balt began to laugh.

Brendt began to panic.

"This isn't bickering, Brendt," Loher laughed.

"Tink o' it like," the dwarf paused to think, "gettin' along."

Brendt looked even more confused.

"Balt likes to fight, and Loher likes to keep him on his toes." Brother Fost finally explained.

"So, it's not fighting?" The sprite asked.

"It is, but it's not." Brother Fost answered.

"I'm confused." Brendt admitted and disappeared.

A faint cheer could be heard from the water as, yet another enemy ship burst into flames, splintered into pieces, and slowly sank into the unforgiving depths.

The ships were close enough to shore for us to roughly make out the shapes of people on the decks of most of the ships.

The sounds of the cannons were unmistakable and with a certain wind direction, we could faintly smell the gunpowder in the air.

I decided to try to count the remaining ships and came up with eighteen ships left, not including The Scorpion.

The sails were missing on two of the three ships closest to The Scorpion and the sails were extremely damaged and on fire on three more ships trying to escape The Scorpion's wrath and get further away.

I was beginning to wonder how The Scorpion was staying intact so well until I finally saw a faint, light blueish green haze around it.

"Kuchoff must be aboard The Scorpion." I pointed out the glow to the rest of my companions.

I wonder if Meeka is with him." Loher commented.

Suddenly a stream of fire erupted from the foremast of the floating golden scorpion and engulfed the sails of yet another enemy ship.

"Aye, Lass," Balt chuckled, "Thar she be."

"I have to admit something," Brother Fost announced.

We all turned to look at the priest.

"I am a bit jealous that they're aboard and we're not."

Balt gently slugged the halfling on the shoulder, "We'll git our turns, Mate."

"I could probably be more useful aboard The Scorpion, healing the wounded." Brother Fost countered.

"If wot-ever's aboard them ships gits ta shore alive," the dwarven warrior offered, "We're prolly gonna need ye 'ere wit us, putin' us back teh-geter."

"Besides," I added, "You get sea-sick too easily."

Balt and Loher both giggled.

"Actually," the priest countered, "I've been getting better."

A barrage of small cannon balls suddenly impacted the beach less than two meters away from where we were standing.

"Those swivel guns have great distance!" Loher shouted and grabbed the priest, dragging him to safety behind a large driftwood tree trunk.

Balt and I dove behind a pile of large rocks.

Moments passed as we sat ducked behind our naturally made barriers, listening to the quickly approaching cannon fire.

"Wot's tat noise?" Balt asked, focusing his senses away from the sea battle and toward the encampment.

I could hear it.

It sounded like pulsing thunder.

Pulsing thunder mixed with melodic, high-pitched tones backed up by erratic hissing.

Without any further introduction or obvious warning, Cirdan and his entire army of eline soldiers suddenly marched into view.

"I t'ought cats were s'post ta be silent hunters," Balt spat in bewilderment.

Dozens of eline soldiers, most dressed in armor, suddenly amassed on the beach and then scattered in all directions with lightning speed.

As they scattered, they blended into the environment around them and seemingly disappeared.

"He's got a lot more soldiers than I thought he did," I admitted.

"Makes me wonder what else he's been hiding," Loher shouted from behind the driftwood stump.

"I don't think they were necessarily hiding," I offered, "Look at the natural skills they possess!"

"Well, I'm glad they're on our side," Brother Fost added with an uneasy pitch in his voice.

"We be useless against tose cannons, Mate," Balt uncharacteristically remarked, returning our attention to the enemy, as he braced himself against the rock and prepared for another barrage of small cannon fire.

This time the cannon balls fell short of even getting close to our hiding areas.

The eline officers advanced closer to us and then began to scatter.

Cirdan ducked behind the boulders that Balt and I were using for cover.

"I'm glad you could join us," I teased.

"They're close enough to make landfall," he commented, "especially if your ship takes another one of theirs out."

"Do you have any idea what Pik has in mind for the errfords?" I asked.

"You mean to join the fight?" Cirdan asked.

"Yes, did he say anything to you about his plans?" I asked.

"Nothing," he stated and peered around the rock to check on the progress of the sea battle, "Is it normal for your ship to glow like that?"

I looked out through a space between two rocks and saw that The Scorpion was surrounded by the remaining ten or so enemy ships.

They were firing their cannons directly at The Scorpion, but the cannonballs were just bouncing off Kuchoff's now bright blueish green Psi-shield that surrounded it, keeping it safe.

I swear I could hear The Scorpion's crew laughing, taunting and jeering the enemy's crews.

"As long as Kuchoff is aboard…" I began as the first wave of enemy soldiers began to wash up on shore.

I needn't say more, as Cirdan nodded his head in understanding.

Loher suddenly appeared beside me, pulling the hood of her cloak from her head, "Hello, Love," she whispered with a smile.

Her cloak opened a bit more and Brother Fost stepped out.

The sudden spectacle startled me, but not as much as it scared Cirdan, who almost literally jumped out of his own skin.

Eline soldiers were already locked in battle with the orc and hobgoblin soldiers.

Periodically, Meeka would cast a stream of fire or magical energy that would erupt from various parts of The Scorpion and engulf part of, or even the entire enemy ship that was being targeted.

(Nine enemy ships)

I could now see that there was a bit of damage to The Scorpion, but nothing, compared to the damage to the rest of the enemy fleet.

Her sails were tattered and torn, and there were freshly patched holes in her already patched sides.

She was still holding her ground against an enemy that outnumbered her eight to one.

(Seven to one)

⸺ ◆ ⸺

We could see the bodies, both living and now, also the dead washing up on shore with the waves.

Pieces of the various enemy ships were washing up with them.

I was about to return Loher's greeting, when I was stopped by a low growl that was steadily growing louder and angrier.

I looked back at Loher who was holding her hands over her ears, her smile began to widen.

I started to understand why she moved.

The growl was almost at a frightening tone when Balt suddenly erupted out from behind his rock.

His battle cry could be heard as he disappeared behind a sand dune and engaged the enemy.

As I strung up my bow and notched in an arrow, I poked Cirdan in the ribs and pointed in the general direction of the upcoming skirmish.

Cirdan rose to his feet, roared out a loud battle cry and rushed into the inevitable action, followed closely by his officers.

"Start chanting your healing juju." Loher granted as she too strung up her bow and started pegging off orcish and hobgoblin marauders.

Brother Fost smiled warily and began audibly chanting while firing off bolts from his Blessed Crossbow.

The sounds of steel on steel suddenly erupted on shore, drowning out Fost's chanting and Balt's war cry.

Balt, eline soldiers and hobgoblin marauders were hand-to-hand, clashing near the shoreline.

The sand and water, becoming stained red from all of the blood.

From my vantage point, I could plainly see Balt in action, so I decided to keep an eye on him and help him out when needed.

My first chance didn't wait too long to present itself as the eline soldier that was fighting next to him fell from a sword thrust through his neck.

The eline corpse fell into the path Balt was taking to evade an oncoming marauder, forcing the dwarf to misstep and trip over it.

Balt was now an easy target for both the marauder coming after him as well as the one that killed the eline.

Assuming that Balt was unaware of the eline's killer and was concentrating on the one he knew was coming after him, I took the shot at the eline killer.

Both marauders fell at Balt's feet.

Balt took a quick look at the situation, raised his Great Axe into the air and let loose an impressive battle cry.

Balt's battle cry struck up lion-like roars from various directions and suddenly, the sounds of battle grew louder and more intense.

My second opportunity to save Balt's life came not with an arrow, but with my blades.

After watching Balt in action for a few years now and especially in this battle, I learned to anticipate his moves.

There was a point in the fight that I knew Balt was eventually going to pass around a large pile of rocks to surprise his next victim, but I knew there was a marauder waiting for him around the corner and he had no idea that it was there.

The marauder was blocked by a rock, and I couldn't get a clear shot with my bow, so I tossed Loher my bow and drew my blades.

I was surprised at how seemingly silent and quick I was as I sprinted toward the rocks.

When I reached the rocks, I quickly turned around and put my back against one and listened.

As I listened, I noticed Loher giving me the 'good to go' signal and I knew from that point on, Loher would protect my back like I was protecting Balt's.

My timing was impeccable; as Balt was just rounding the corner and the hobgoblin was about to attack, I gently slid the blade of the eline short sword through the base of its skull and twisted the blade.

The blade went in cleanly and easily, as if it...belonged in there.

The hobgoblin corpse crumpled to the ground with a loud thud and a ringing clang from its sword bouncing against the rock.

"Oi, McLaaud," Balt greeted, un-startled.

"Balt," I acknowledged, nodding my head once at him.

"Tat one yers 'r mine?" he asked.

"Mine." I answered.

"I'll git ta next'n," he assured.

I was about to playfully disagree with him when he suddenly narrowed his eyes...

"Duck n roll left," he calmly commanded.

I ducked and then I rolled left.

There was a wet thud directly behind my head.

I rolled over once more so I'd be facing in the other direction.

What I saw when my eyes came into focus, was the head of a hobgoblin laying where my own head once was a few seconds ago.

It was staring me right in the eyes as if we were lying peacefully in the sand together.

A small amount of vomit found its way up my throat and into my mouth.

I choked it back down and took a deep breath.

"Telled ya," the dwarf laughed and offered a hand to help me to my feet.

I thanked him by punching him in the shoulder and then we both turned in opposite directions in search of our next victims.

He trekked further into the battlefield, as I returned to my bow.

The sun was almost directly overhead at this point and the heat and humidity mixture was almost unbearable.

The cannon fire was louder than ever as the battling ships were close enough to be in danger of beaching.

Once again, from my vantage point, I could see that The Scorpion was only outnumbered three to one now, but the Psi-shield's glow was growing faint.

"Kuchoff must be getting tired," I mentioned to Loher as I motioned toward The Scorpion.

"Meeka will know what to do," she assured and loosed another arrow with a satisfied grin.

I looked around and noticed, "Where's Fost?" I asked.

Loher pointed to a small area off to the side of the beach battle, "Healing soldiers." She chuckled, "He must be doing a great job, look at all of those flashes."

I took a closer look, "some of those flashes are nowhere near him," I corrected, "and besides, his healing doesn't flash like that."

"Then there must be a mage or something down there with them," Loher breathed as she swiftly rose to a crouching position, "we need to investigate."

Another wave of cheering abruptly wafted from the decks of The Scorpion as they were left with only two enemy ships, but Kuchoff's Psi-shield was no longer glowing, and I began to become concerned.

Loher and I drew our blades, turned toward the skirmish and began to jog; we wanted to keep an eye on where or what those flashes were coming from.

As we entered the battlefront, we noticed that the dead were all hobgoblins with a few orcs mixed in for good measure.

We also noticed that the only eline corpses that we could find were pretty mangled up and barely recognizable.

We rounded the rock that Brother Fost was behind and saw dozens of errfords healing the injured.

"These guys are really good," Loher remarked.

"Apparently," I agreed, "I'm glad they're on our side."

"I knew you were going to say that." Loher laughed.

"Orc to your right," I calmly warned.

Loher sheathed her sword and drew her bow, "Easy pickings," she half whispered as she notched an arrow to the string.

Seemingly without aiming, Loher drew back the string and just as quickly let the arrow fly.

Her arrow found purchase in the center of its pig-like nose and the orc dropped to the ground after taking three more running steps.

"Dammit!" Balt yelled and then appeared from behind a chunk of washed-up driftwood, "Tat one was supposta be mine!"

"Go find another one!" Loher yelled back at him, teasing.

"Tere ain't no more, look!" Balt shouted and flayed his arm over the scene.

We looked around and noticed that all the survivors were eline, gathered in groups around more of the errford flashing.

"Oh good, you two," Brother Fost sighed, "I know I probably shouldn't, but I feared for your lives."

"Fost," I excitedly greeted, "what is all of this?"

"Errfords!" The priest smiled, "They've been helping me heal the wounded."

"So tey actually did sumptin ta 'elp us after all." Balt jeered.

"We heal," a voice with an uncharacteristically high pitched Dwarven accent said from apparently behind Brother Fost.

Brother Fost turned around and we saw nothing.

"In my hood," the priest added.

Nestled into the hood of Brother Fost's priestly robes, was an errford, except this one was grey.

"We heal," the errford repeated with an Elven accent this time.

"This is Nitch," Fost introduced, "he is one of the errford elders, which is why I'm protecting him in my hood."

"He doesn't have to protect me," Nitch commented, "he thinks he does, but..." the errford's voice trailed off.

"It turns out," Fost excitedly began, "whenever an errford heals an eline that eline inherits the power to heal as well."

"That's exciting news!" Loher agreed.

"Can the eline transfer that magic between others?" I asked, intrigued.

Loher began to look off into the distance with an odd look on her face, "The Scorpion is getting awfully close to—."

Brother Fost and Nitch suddenly disappeared in a puff of pink smoke.

We looked up at The Scorpion and saw the same pink smoke drifting upon her deck.

"They probably need medical help," I suggested, "earlier, I noticed Kuchoff's Psi-shield was weakening and then just before we went down the hill into battle, I saw that his shield was gone."

⚬

The Scorpion made her way back out to the open sea, trying to entice the marauders to follow her instead of making landfall.

"Whatever they're doing over there," I began, "they'd better do it quickly, that ship is heading right for them."

"What's the other one doing?" Loher asked as she examined the contents of yet another dead hobgoblin's purse.

"Repairing their sails," I observed.

By this time the sun was already dipping behind some low laying clouds on the horizon, making it seem like an early dusk.

The silhouettes of the opposing ships danced around on the watery stage as they bobbed up and down on the increasing waves.

"Flamin' arrows," Balt calmly reported as he happened to look up from the weapons he had gathered to inspect and perhaps keep.

He has kept various weapons that he has found in just about every fight he has been in.

His arsenal was huge and only getting bigger.

"They've been trying that for a while now," I remarked, finding myself growing bored of the ship race, "they're still too far away to find their targets."

"What's Cirdan doing?" Loher asked after a few minutes of silence.

"Round'n up ta troops," Balt slowly guessed as he intently wondered at a dagger in his pile, "I would be if I was 'im."

After a long moment and without any warning, a long steady burst of flames from the deck of The Scorpion shot across the water and engulfed the approaching ship as soon as it was within range.

Loher and I gasped in shock and awe.

"Dammit!" Balt swore, "An' when I be lookin' down too."

I took a closer look at The Scorpion and noticed that there was a new glow around her, only this time, it was the same light blue glow of the errford self -preservation shield instead of the greenish blue glow of Kuchoff's Psi-shield.

"Way to go, Little Fur-ball," I thought aloud and sighed a breath of relief.

"The eline are getting ready for another wave of enemy," Loher casually reported.

"T'at's great!" Balt exclaimed, now with a renewed sense of purpose, "A chance ta try out tis beauty," Balt smiled and wielded a large, curved dagger.

"Have fun," I playfully called after him as he walked toward the beach.

"Try to keep your boots dry," Loher teased.

Balt spat something that we couldn't understand back at us as he put on his helmet and began to jog.

Knowing Balt the way we do; it was probably something sarcastic.

As we watched our warrior friend jovially jog away, we were distracted by yet another fan of both cannon fire, as well as magical fire, erupt from the decks of The Scorpion as it passed the last remaining ship.

"DAMMIT!" we heard Balt yell from the moderate distance he was away, "Missed seein' anot'er one!"

"They're much too far away from shore for any of them to survive," I informed as we watched the final ship sink into the vast sea.

Loher only smiled as she began to walk toward the beach.

A heavy burst of cheering erupted from the decks of the champion ship, The Scorpion, but it was swiftly drowned out by the increasing winds.

As I caught up to her, I noticed that the blue glow was gone, and The Scorpion had already turned around and began to head back to shore.

The wind was noticeably stronger as the next wave of surviving marauders reached the shore.

Eline soldiers quickly overtook the invaders, and it was over as fast as it began.

"Tis seems all too familiar," Balt morbidly expressed as the clouds began to close in.

"What do you mean?" Loher asked as she secured her hair from blowing in her face.

"When tat ship attacked Ta Scorpion an wot got us stuck 'ere in ta first place," Balt began, "it started off juss like tis."

Just then, I happened to look up at The Scorpion and saw that she was maneuvering to get into position beside the rocky point, like a natural pier or dock.

I was becoming relieved that they were only moments away from being safely back ashore, when suddenly and violently, the largest and brightest lightning bolt I have ever witnessed came crashing down upon The Scorpion, setting her sails ablaze and knocking her off course and into the jutting rocks of the natural dock.

Out of the dark clouds that were quickly rolling in, appeared a giant ship, twice the size of The Scorpion.

Immediately, bright white balls of energy began to spray from the decks of the enormous ship, barraging The Scorpion.

Splinters of flaming wood exploded into the air.

The splinters mixed into the increasing wind and began to blow around, creating spears and other impaling hazards for both our companions and crew aboard The Scorpion, but for us as well, as a large splinter of what looked to be a piece of her claw, came within centimeters of impaling Loher in the leg.

My first thoughts went out to Brother Fost, Meeka and Kuchoff, followed closely by Captain Mario Waxx and his crew.

Then I remembered Nitch, the innocent errford elder in Fost's hood.

They have the natural ability to shield the area around themselves in case of danger.

Perhaps if he is still in the priest's hood, he would cloak them both, leaving the pair of them to help and heal the rest.

Better than I suspected, Nitch's self-preservation shield suddenly surrounded what was left of The Scorpion and the enemy energy balls began to bounce harmlessly off and fall sizzling into the sea.

Next, a volley of Meeka's deadly accurate fireballs successfully found their targets aboard the enemy ship.

They must have decided that Meeka's magic was more powerful than they had anticipated, because their own version of a protection field abruptly appeared around the exposed, closer portion of their ship, leaving the further half of the ship still exposed.

Another volley of mixed energy-balls and Meeka's fireballs spewed forth between the opposing ships, both bouncing harmlessly off and dying in the sea.

Apparently realizing that they could do no further harm to the already disabled Scorpion without potentially harming themselves in the process, the enemy ship turned course for shore.

"Tey plan to make land an fight us from tere," Balt surmised.

The enemy ship swung around between the shoreline and The Scorpion, always keeping their protection shield on the side facing The Scorpion.

I jabbed Loher in the ribs with the end of my bow as I began to notch an arrow to the string, "I'm not sure if I can hit anything from here, but with your new bow, I am sure that you can."

"Earlier, I noticed a few eline with bows," she smiled, "let's see if they're still around."

The eline archers weren't very difficult to find, we just had to think like a cat and look for the tallest or highest vantage point, which was...

...the crow's nest on the wreckage of the messenger ship from a few days earlier.

As we arrived aboard the messenger ship, we were greeted by friendly eager eline soldiers.

They told us that there was no more room up in the crow's nest, but we were more than welcome to stay and fight from there.

The vantage point was better than it had to be, because in just a few short moments, the enemy ship should be facing us broadside with their shields between them and The Scorpion, leaving their exposed side closer to us.

We had just enough time to relay a message to the crow's nest about our plans. If we can take some of them out and weaken them enough with our arrows, perhaps Meeka could get past their shield with a strong enough fireball and light them ablaze.

The plan was set, and everything was in order in hopes that Meeka would take the advantage when given.

The enemy ship was finally in range and with one perfectly aimed flaming arrow launched from Loher's new Bow of Accuracy as the signal, the smoke-filled sky suddenly darkened with hundreds of arrows raining down upon the enemy ship.

Sounds of not only the screams of dying hobgoblins and orcs rang out, but we could hear the unmistakable screams of humans as well.

The wind suddenly completely stopped.

Silence.

The magical shield on the enemy ship began to fade away until it was barely visible.

"Come on, Meeka," Loher breathed, "take the shot."

The Scorpion's cannon fire sounded like the thunder that should have followed the lightning flash that started this whole battle off.

The angle and power of the point-blank cannonball hits from The Scorpion literally tore the enemy ship into pieces sending smoldering shards of sharp wood, a large cache of bladed weapons and hundreds of hobgoblin and orc bodies into the air and surrounding sea.

Somehow, in the chaos, a pair of human magic practitioners managed to escape on a lifeboat or dingy and were floating out of harm's way waiting to see what was about to unfold next upon the beach.

Loher tried to reach them with her bow and arrows but fell just shy of her target.

The wizards began to jeer and taunt her in an apparent attempt to distract or anger her.

Moments later, hundreds of hobgoblins, orcs and a spattering of humans began to wash up on shore.

The adjacent shoreline near the rocky point suddenly began to fill with pink mist while the beach began to fill with the sounds and deeds of steel-on-steel fighting.

"Everybody, grab an errford!" Brother Fost commanded as loud as he could, as soon as the pink mist was thin enough to see through, "They'll protect you!"

I instantly began running up the beach toward them; Loher was right behind me.

Once we had sand and stone beneath our feet, we began to sprint across the battlefield toward our friends.

The metallic odor of fresh blood began to emanate from the carnage.

We could plainly see Meeka and Kuchoff casting low energy fireballs at their land-based attackers which were mostly hobgoblins.

Occasionally, out of the corner of my eye, I would catch the sight of an eline, carrying an errford, fighting an orc or a hobgoblin, the protective blue glow surrounding the goodish pair.

I had to stop my running short as I had noticed that Loher was starting to lag behind, which was highly unusual.

As I jogged at a slower pace for her to catch up, an eline soldier cut down an orc marauder so close to me that I could feel and taste the spray of blood against my skin.

"Is that your blood?" Loher asked as she approached and slowed down.

I shook my head, telling her no and then pointed back at the dead orc.

She nodded her head in recognition and continued to keep up with my lessened speed.

Moments later, we arrived at the scene where Brother Fost was healing Meeka's shoulder, a bloody dagger and a severely mangled, yet still living orc lying at Kuchoff's feet.

I could tell that Kuchoff's magical and Psionic energy was severely weakened, so I reminded him of the legendary Shino Sutoka Katana he had strapped to his back.

The young man smiled nervously, and unsheathed his new weapon, looked up at me and then back to his weapon.

His ever-present goofy toothy grin widened on his face but then was quickly washed away by tears.

As if he had practiced with that very sword for his whole entire life, in one fluid motion, Kuchoff suddenly beheaded the mangled beast at his feet, wiped the blade clean and then returned it to its sheath.

No one was shocked.

Very proud, but not shocked.

My attention was caught by the bloody dagger lying next to the now deceased orc and then back up to Meeka's now healed and patched up shoulder, "Is this your first stab wound?"

"She thought she was invincible," Kuchoff tattled as he reached down and retrieved the dagger.

"Let me explain," Meeka cut in, shooting Kuchoff a scolding glance, "I was experimenting with the wand that Loher found on the wreckage and discovered, lucky for me, that I am invincible from magic while in possession of this wand."

"Tell them how you discovered it," Kuchoff prodded and handed her the dagger.

"Yes, please tell us," Brother Fost softly demanded with his arms crossed over his puffed-out chest and stressed out look on his face.

"I was hit with an energy-ball, and it just bounced off with no effects," the wizardess confessed, trying to sound nonchalant.

"You could have been killed!" Loher cried and took a slight step toward Meeka.

Meeka took a full step away, frowned and put up her hands as if to ward off Loher's slight advance, "I've already heard enough of it from Captain Waxx. Please don't."

Loher eased away gracefully and turned to look at me.

—◆—

"Isn't that Balt?" Kuchoff asked as he narrowed his eyes in a feeble attempt to see through the drifting and blowing smoke-filled darkness of dusk.

"Yes," Brother Fost agreed, "It looks like he's yelling something, but he's too far to hear."

"Like we would even understand his accent at this distance," Loher laughed.

"Yer missin' all ta fun, Mates, come git ye some." I repeated, suddenly surprised that I heard him as well as I did.

"How did you hear him so well?" Loher asked, obviously as surprised as I was, "I'm full elf and even I couldn't hear a thing above the fighting."

I just shrugged my shoulders, shook my head and looked back over at Balt, who was now running toward us.

In the falling darkness, the firelight was starting to dance on the water, creating a wavy eerie orangish shimmer to the already blood-soaked sand of the beach.

The wind had died down to a light breeze, returning the waves to their usual size.

The oblong shadows of the fighting foes that were cast off in all different directions by the various fires, began to grow and dance the all too familiar flickering fire dance.

Occasionally, a random fireball or energy-ball would whizz by and explode off something, or someone, creating a break in the seduction of the dance, violently tearing you back into the grim reality of war.

"We need ta git back innare!" Balt called frantically, losing the little bit of patience that he already didn't have.

"We might as well," I said to my companions and nodded toward the action.

"Everyone, grab an errford," Fost futilely reminded, his words trailing off into the growing smog of the battlefield.

We all got up and began to run toward Balt, who, by this time had stopped and began kicking in the skull of a fallen...unidentifiable creature, as he waited.

As we arrived, an energy-ball suddenly exploded in the sand about two meters away from the dwarven warrior, kicking us all into a sudden excitement.

"They know we're out here now," Kuchoff stated, gripping the hilt of his katana.

"Guid," The dwarf grunted and began to trot toward the fighting crowds.

Kuchoff looked at me with a look of half amusement, half worry on his face as he too began to quicken his pace toward the brawl.

I've watched Kuchoff grow from a young boy with the greatest potential and the biggest, goofiest toothy grin that I had ever seen, into a young man; an exceptionally skilled protégé, that I saw then, at that moment as he followed his best friend, the dwarven warrior, into battle.

"Meeka and I are going to stay here," Fost announced, "Nitch will keep us safe."

Nitch finally poked his head out of Fost's hood at the sound of his name.

"Keep them safe for me," I requested of the errford elder.

"Stay safe yourself," the elder agreed, in the Elven tongue, with a very charming, human-like smile.

I turned and looked back at my companions and saw that they had started off without me.

"Kuchoff?" Meeka reached out to me weakly.

"Go," Fost quietly urged as he took Meeka by the wrist and began to lead her to a safer area.

"I'll bring him back alive," I vowed as I turned on my heel, digging into the sand and began to sprint effortlessly toward my battle buddies.

My strides were swift, and it seemed like I was running on air.

["I'll make you pay with your soul, Ranger!"]

An image of the tavern, that night, so long ago invaded my mind...

...Yet I had no dark hunger.

That sudden taste of blood that sprayed into my mouth didn't seem to tempt me.

I felt alive – more than alive, I felt reborn.

Chapter Eight

MOMENTUM DEFINIENS

Apparently, none of my companions noticed that I had lagged behind as I caught up to them faster than I would have without my re-found vampiric enhancements.

I noticed that the enhancements showed up in spurts, usually whenever I became excited or anxious, and they would last just long enough for me to accomplish whatever it was that I needed them for.

I could run faster and longer, my hearing is more acute, my physical strength far exceeds what it was before the vampire attack.

I was sure that it wouldn't be long before I had to start explaining the return of what I would now consider 'gifts' instead of a potential curse.

Within moments, I caught up to my friends.

We had decided to hide behind the large group of rocks and driftwood that we had utilized in the recent past and wait for an opportune time to engage the enemy.

Hiding somewhere nearby, our magic wielding foes were watching and waiting for one of us to make a mistake and show ourselves.

I gathered the attention of my companions, "Do you remember when I was a vampire?" I asked.

They all agreed that they did, with varying reactions to the question.

Loher grimaced as she kicked away a rat.

"Do you remember that I could run faster and hear better than the rest of you?"

They all agreed.

"And that I was stronger and..."

"What'r ye tryn'ta tell us, McLaaud?" Balt spat and kicked away another rat.

I pulled the hood of my invisibility cloak over my head as I stated, "All of those abilities are back," and then disappeared.

I didn't want to witness their reactions, so I edged out past the safety of our rocks and slowly ventured out into danger.

Step one – still alive.

I looked to see if I could locate the caster of energy-balls but was unsuccessful.

Step two – still alive.

I ventured out a little further, still not convinced that I could not be seen, as our foes may in fact be invisible as well.

Step three – Still alive, feeling a bit more confident.

Rats scurried over my boot.

I slowly made my way around the rocks to see if I could catch a glimpse of who or what was directly on the other side from my companions.

Steps four, five and six – I found myself face to face with an aging greying human male, obviously unaware of my presence.

He was wearing the same style and color of robes that the original human was wearing when we first got stuck in this realm.

The man leaned forward to try to sneak a peek around the rock to see if perhaps one of us was doing the same.

I silently drew my eline short sword and gently held the edge of the blade across the back of his neck without touching him.

The man kicked a rat and then stretched out a slight bit more to try to get a better look.

I tightened my grip on the handle and held the blade to his throat while pressing my other hand into the small of his back.

"Don't, move, a muscle," I slowly growled into his ear.

The sudden unmistakable odor of human urine filled the air.

"You can come out now," I called to my team as I removed my hood.

An arrow noisily bounced off my chest plate, "On second thought," I spat as I too, ducked back behind the rocks, still grasping my prisoner.

Loher and Kuchoff suddenly appeared next to me again.

"Is this going to become a habit?" I teased.

"Where did this arrow come from?" Loher rhetorically asked as she inspected the projectile that bounced off my chest.

"And what did you mean when you said, all of those abilities are back?" Kuchoff asked with a slight frown on his face, instead of his usual toothy grin.

"I've been noticing that my hearing, my sense of smell, my eyesight in both light and darkness and my strength and speed have been slowly returning from when I was undead," I explained, "but with no dark hunger. I'm not craving blood."

The prisoner began to struggle so I tightened my grip and squeezed his arm until he said, "Ow."

"The sight and smell of blood doesn't make me want to drink it at all," I reaffirmed.

I decided to leave the accidental tasting part out.

The human prisoner relaxed a bit after hearing that information.

Kuchoff's reaction was favorable as his slight frown became more of a grin.

Balt, now present, however, was staring at me with a steady eye, "I gots me eye on ye," he warned sternly.

"I'm counting on it, my friend," I immediately acknowledged with respect and offered my hand in friendship.

The dwarf instantly smiled, grabbed my hand and pulled me in for an awkward hug.

The prisoner groaned.

Loher was silent and looked worried but still managed to show me a trusting smile.

"What are we going to do with him?" Kuchoff asked, motioning toward the human prisoner.

"I don't know," I admitted, "too bad there's no brig on The Scorpion."

"There is," Kuchoff commented, "maybe Meeka could blink him to the brig."

"She's just over there," Loher agreed.

"Come on," I commanded the prisoner, and began to head back to Meeka.

The prisoner gave us no trouble as we made our way back to Meeka's hiding place.

Within moments, our prisoner was safely aboard The Scorpion and in the brig.

"Are we gonna go git ta bastards 'r' wot?" Balt growled and bounced the flat side of his Great Axe's blade off the front of his helmet with a clang.

Kuchoff secured his katana to his back and unsheathed the weapon.

"Bows?" Loher asked as she notched an arrow to her string.

I only smiled as I drew my long sword and raised my hood back over my head.

The elven maiden smiled back and pulled her own hood over her head, leaned in and kissed me, "Don't die."

I turned to Balt and Kuchoff, "Don't worry about where I am, I'll keep an eye on you."

"Aye, Mate," Balt grunted and then proceeded into what I choose to believe is his 'happy place.'

"Won't Loher hit you with an arrow?" Kuchoff asked, "You're invisible."

"Loher is wearing her cloak as well, so she will be able to see me," I reassured.

Kuchoff just nodded his head in my direction and promptly followed the warrior into the unforgiving heart of combat.

⸺⬦⸺

The first opponent that Balt ran into was an already half burned half dead hobgoblin.

Balt decided to have mercy and put the poor creature out of its misery with a quick thrust of his 'new' curved dagger.

The dwarf looked over at Kuchoff and said, "I gonna call tis, 'Ta hobby-goblin hobbler'," as he showed off the blade he had just used.

"Why do you want to call it that?" Kuchoff asked as he slid his own blade across the belly of an unsuspecting orc, nearly slicing it in two.

"Find me a hobby-goblin an I'll show ye." Balt answered as he scouted out the area, already overpopulated with corpses.

Kuchoff suddenly tripped over the body of a hobgoblin.

"Ta footin' gits a bit tricky," Balt laughed, "ye'll git used ta it."

The young man successfully righted himself just in time to see a pair of hobgoblins rushing right toward them, "There we go," Kuchoff called and pointed at the foes and readied his blade.

"I'll take ta one on ta left," Balt called as he rushed in.

I could see that the boy was having a difficult time maneuvering through the bodies, so I wound my way toward the enemy on the right, in case Balt needed the cover.

"Keep yer eyes on tis, Boy-o!" Balt called as he gracefully rolled behind his advancing attacker and sliced the back of the hobgoblin's knees at the joint.

The beast lunged uncontrollably forward and then toppled over, bleeding out and howling out in pain and frustration as it quickly died.

Kuchoff's katana also found blood as it sliced cleanly through his enemy's arm and straight through the ribs and lungs, finally coming to a dead stop on the spine.

Blood sprayed from the monster's mouth and nose as it dropped its sword and clutched at its nonexistent arm.

Kuchoff yanked out the blade and spun around to encounter yet another hobgoblin, which dumbly impaled itself on the katana's blade.

"Verra guid," Balt commended, "Yer a natural!"

Un-phased by Balt's complement, the young man concentrated on staying vertical and began to stand on the backs and heads of the fallen, despite what race it was, although the dead marauders outnumbered the dead eline approximately thirty to one.

I suddenly found myself in an odd predicament as another younger human male stumbled into view.

He was obviously wearing some sort of invisibility charm, because he didn't look concerned when he saw Balt and Kuchoff.

I'm not sure if he realized that I was cloaked, as he probably saw me as well, but I didn't give him the chance to give it a second thought.

I ran at him as fast as my vampiric enhancements would carry me and dove for his legs.

My body's impact with his knees sent us both tumbling down a sand dune.

I tried to grab a hold of him but was a few centimeters short and pulled back a handful of sand.

At the bottom of the dune, I found my new prisoner trying to chant some sort of spell while trying to crawl away on broken legs.

I must have grabbed him up before he could complete the spell because as I lifted him off the ground, I heard a slight fizzle and quiet pop along with a tiny puff of dark pinkish smoke.

Rats scattered around my feet from the noise of the sudden pop.

With the knowledge of us both being invisible, I carried him to Meeka and had her strip him of any magical possessions and blink him to the brig on The Scorpion as well.

Back in the bloody grind of warfare, I stayed invisible and found Kuchoff in the middle of a battle with two orcs.

I notched an arrow to my bow and readied it on the orc Kuchoff was not directly engaged with, in case he needed help.

I waited to fire because I was curious about how well he could handle this situation.

It turned out he handled it with ease as he neutralized the first orc and within the same fluid motion, decapitated the second.

I then turned around to find myself chest to face with Balt as he was trying to evade an oncoming ogre.

"Where did that ogre come from?" I shouted into the air as I pulled off my hood.

"Dunno, Mate," Balt called back with a slight song in his rough voice, "but 'e' makes a great dancin' partner!"

Balt lifted his Great Axe and was about ready to strike the killing blow to the ogre, when a sudden energy-ball impacted with the Axe blade, knocking the weapon from the dwarf's hands.

Balt growled and dove away from the oncoming beastie and sought after his Axe.

I looked into the general area that I last saw the dingy carrying the pair of magical practitioners and noticed that they too, were on the beach, walking slowly toward my group and me.

Periodically, one or both would cast an energy-ball at anything that got too close to them, but always keeping a steady eye on us.

The ogre skidded to a stop and proceeded to dive on top of our dwarven hero.

The younger of the two conjurors produced a scroll or some sort of parchment from the folds of his robe and proceeded to read the words aloud.

Gradually, starting off as a dull yellow, a glow began to emanate from around the caster, slowly brightening as the spell was repeated.

With each time repeated, the glow would grow a little brighter.

I noticed that Balt was lying motionless in the sand, his hand, resting just within reach of his Great Axe handle.

Kuchoff and the ogre were nowhere to be seen.

"Meeka is going to kill me," I thought to myself as I tried to move closer to Balt, but found that my movements were impaired, "if these guys don't do it for her."

I was moving slower than I did, even in my half elven state and I deduced that the yellow glow from the young sorcerer must be the reason why.

"If this is affecting my movements this way," I thought, "this has got to be the reason Balt isn't moving either. I have got to do something about that human."

With every bit of energy I could gather, I began to move at almost my normal rate toward the human men and just as I was about to attack the glowing yellow one, an arrow suddenly found itself buried in my shoulder.

The impact of the arrow spun me around and thrust me into the elder of the two men, knocking us both to the ground.

As I tried to regain my composure and attempted to pin my foe to the ground, another arrow came flitting over my head and into the face of the glowing man.

The yellow glow began to rapidly fade as the man crumpled lifeless to the ground.

"Dammit," I cursed, "I wanted him alive."

With my returning vampiric strength, I effortlessly pinned my still living and breathing prisoner to the ground.

"Don't kill me!" The old man pled, "I can send you home."

I eased up on the frail old wizard.

"There is a wand hidden aboard that ship," he said, pointing at the wreckage from the day before, "the wand," he gasped, "It will take you home."

I quickly searched the old man for any magical trinkets that he could possibly use against me and stripped him of all his rings and charms.

"Dammit," Balt cursed, "ta war's over and you got ta last baddie."

"We're keeping this one alive," I demanded as I lifted the wizard to his feet, "He's got some valuable information that Meeka will definitely want to hear."

"An t'en we kill 'im," Balt spat.

"Balt," I shot with a scolding tone.

"Wot?"

"We're not going to kill him," I repeated and started to guide the old man toward the camp.

"Yet," Balt mumbled as he let the old man pass.

"Balt?" I asked.

"Wot now??" Balt asked, convinced that I was going to scold him again.

"Where's Kuchoff?" I asked, looking around.

"Where's ta ogre?" He asked in return, also looking around.

We both frantically began looking around for our missing companion without calling out his name, for we didn't want Meeka to know that he was missing.

The minutes seemed to go on forever until...

"... What are you guys looking for?" Kuchoff asked as he appeared from within the hazy depths of the smog.

"We're looking for you," I sighed in relief at the sight of the kid unharmed.

"Where'd tat ogre run off ta?" Balt interrupted.

Kuchoff smiled and hooked his thumb over his shoulder, "In that direction, in about six or seven pieces," he smiled and then said excitedly, "I love this sword."

I smiled and playfully slugged him on the shoulder as he walked past me to go check on Meeka.

"I am so sorry about your shoulder, McLaaud," Loher apologized as we arrived close to where she had stationed herself.

"Awe...Sumptin' wrong wit yer shoulder?" Balt asked me, teasing Loher, "I didn't notice ta arrow juttin' outta ya."

"Don't die?" I reminded her sarcastically and kissed her.

"I didn't kill you, did I?" Loher defended and playfully shoved me away.

"She's wearing her hood, you said," Kuchoff quipped, "She'll see me, you said."

I started laughing.

Without warning, Loher grabbed the arrow and gave it a swift tug.

⁜

I woke up aboard The Scorpion shortly after the sun had come up with a stiff soreness in my shoulder.

"There was no damage to my arrow," Loher mentioned with a satisfied sigh and then giggled, "I've been waiting hours to tell you that."

"Hours?" I echoed.

"You passed out from the pain of me yanking the arrow out of your shoulder.

"It hurt," I admitted, "horribly."

"I truly am sorry for shooting you." Loher apologized.

"I think you might have actually saved my life," I thanked with a chuckle, "and the old man's as well, which reminds me, Meeka, did you get any information from him?"

"Balt and Kuchoff are still talking to the trio of humans," she said, "they've been over there for hours and things seem to be going well. Balt sometimes looks bored or confused, but it seems like they're getting along well enough."

"Believe it or not," she changed the subject, "Brother Fost started teaching Kuchoff how to properly use that sword."

I smiled and nodded my head.

"How would a halfling priest know anything about using an assassin's katana?" Loher genuinely asked.

"Brother Fost probably isn't teaching him how to kill with it," I explained, "he's probably teaching him how to become one with the sword and make it an extension of his own body and mind," I paused, "or some other mysteriousness like that."

Some time passed by as Loher inspected the bandage on my shoulder and then turned to inspect the bandage on Meeka's shoulder, "McLaaud," she said, breaking the silence, "what are your plans after we return to Beornan Heafod?"

"Besides the obvious reporting to our King, I haven't given it much thought," I answered, "perhaps I'll ask you to marry me."

Meeka's eyes widened and she began to smile.

Loher's smile widened and she began to cry.

Meeka's smile widened and she began to cry.

Balt just happened to walk up and notice the girls crying, "'e's dead?" he asked in a sudden panic not able to see me behind them, "Wot 'appened? Ya killt 'im?"

Balt paced the floor, waving his hands in the air, "It was just a arrow in ta shoulder," he ranted, "tat shuldn'ta killt 'im!"

"I'm fine, Balt," I called and sat up.

"Wot? Why are tey cryin' fer?" Balt stammered in confusion.

"He just asked Loher to marry him," Meeka sniffled between sobs.

The dwarven warrior stood there silently as if he was searching for something to say, "Guid ta see ya back on yer feets again, McLaaud," is all Balt growled as he turned around and walked away, grumbling something under his breath.

"Meeka," I called, interrupting the girls' 'moment', "The old man told me something about that wand you have, being able to send us back to our own realm.

Do you know anything about what he might be saying?"

"No," she answered with renewed excitement, "I think I'm well enough to go talk to him now," she said as she got up and brushed herself off, "congratulations you two!"

"For what?" Loher asked.

"You're getting married, Silly!" The wizardess gushed and pranced away.

"Did someone mention a wedding?" Brendt sang as he flitted around and finally came to a rest on a shelf near my head, "I L.O.V.E. weddings! Who's getting married?"

"No one," I answered sardonically, "if we can't get back to our own realm."

"Well sure you could," the sprite chirped, pantomiming the action of sprinkling sand over the situation, "Brother Fost could conduct the ritual," he said as he buzzed past my ear, "Balt could be your best man," he said as he buzzed past my other ear, "and Kuchoff could be the flower—" Brendt stopped and landed back on the shelf with a dramatic twist of his torso as he noticed the unchanging frown upon my face.

He put his hands on his hips and huffed a big sigh, "Look McLaaud," he said as he hopped down to my shoulder, "there's plenty of nice places to live around here, well, there's the..." he stopped in thought, "no, but there's the..." The sprite cupped his hand on his chin and began to think and after a while, "Sorry Buddy, I guess we're just going to have to get you all back home."

"How do you propose we do that?" I asked.

"I have an idea; I'll be back soon!" The sprite said with a flail of his arms and then disappeared.

I got up from my resting place against the wall and slowly began to walk toward the mess hall and the rest of my team.

The sailors and some of the eline were busy repairing The Scorpion while the errfords did what they could to help, but unfortunately, they were only getting in the way.

It was amazing to see an errford with every single sailor and soldier.

Occasionally, a light blue flash would be seen from somewhere around the vicinity of The Scorpion, which only reinforced Brother Fost's earlier report of a decline in injuries.

My team members and I each were chosen by our own errford companion, although I wouldn't be able to tell the name of the one that chose me.

I'm fairly sure he or she was completely terrified of me.

As I walked through the ship, I overheard bits and pieces of conversations, mere idle chatter of plans for a few eline soldiers preparing to ask if they could join our team.

Other conversations were about the possible upcoming wedding.

(I let that slip terribly.)

The most important conversation started as soon as I arrived in the mess hall, with Loher, Meeka, Balt and Kuchoff.

A small crowd of interested sailors and eline soldiers had gathered around.

Errfords dotted the surrounding nooks and crannies as well as sitting on people's heads and shoulders.

CHAPTER NINE

PROPE EST

Meeka was holding the wand that Loher had found aboard the earlier messenger ship that we had destroyed in the cove a few days ago.

Her green eyes seemed to glow among the fiery red hair that surrounded her face as it flowed in semi-tight curls down to her shoulders and beyond.

Her face had shown a proud look unlike any other that I had ever seen there before.

"I hold here, the key to our future," she proudly began as she held the wand in the air, "In exchange for his life and those of his companions, we have made a deal with Lemac, one of the wizards that McLaaud had captured."

Meeka nodded at me, and I smiled and waved my fingers in the air.

Realizing I felt and looked like a fool, I quickly hid my hand, smiled and turned back to Meeka.

"We have decided to hold Lemac and his companions as sort of prisoners until they can be tried and sentenced by our King, Lagu Ofer'Eal," Meeka continued, "In exchange for this, Lemac has instructed me in the ways of this wand and I can now get us, The Scorpion and her crew, back home to the Realm of Beornan Heafod!"

A murmurous buzz of excitement ebbed within the crowd.

"Wot 'r we waitn' fer?" Balt bellowed.

"De Scorpion is still a little sick, Bruddah," Captain Waxx answered from the crowd, "Just a few mar days an' we'll be right on it, Mon."

"Ta man wit ta plan," Balt laughed and slapped his knee, "Wot kin I do ta help ye?"

"I be hearin' dat ya be good wit fixin' an' sharpinin' tools," the captain replied.

"Show me what'cha gots," Balt offered as he escorted the captain out of the room.

⚬

Less than one week later, the repairs to The Scorpion were finally complete and we were more than ready and eager to depart back to charted waters.

I was finishing up with some last-minute packing before I was to dismantle the tent that Loher and I had shared, when there was a sudden presence of three eline soldiers at my doorway.

I turned around and faced the door and instantly recognized the face of my friend, Commander Cirdan.

With him were two of his most trusted lieutenants, yet they were not the same two that I had originally met in the camp.

He introduced each of them in the order of their place within the pride.

His second, a seven-foot tall, black and gray striped, fur covered-rock- was named Rion.

Rion was a ferocious fighter, more brawn and brute force than stealth and stalking.

He preferred to wield a short sword in one hand and a medium sized shield in the other if he decided to use weapons at all.

Quick, extremely large and powerful.

Cirdan's third, Roash, was quite a bit shorter than Rion and nowhere near as big.

Speed and stealth were this one's game.

Sleek, muscular and completely shadow black and grey, Roash was difficult to see in the daylight shadows, not to mention she was virtually invisible in the dark of night.

Roash wasn't very talkative, but she was very expressive in her posture and reactions.

Her weapons of choice were a set of custom-made iron claws that attach to her wrists and ankles, along with dual blades, one in each hand.

I quickly realized that she was the same eline I had seen flipping around the heads of our enemy the day before.

She also liked to play with daggers.

"I am humbled by your presence," I greeted with a low bow.

"We came here to ask you for a favor," Cirdan announced officially.

"May I guess what that favor might be?" I asked.

Surprised by my unexpected question, the eline commander stuttered, "G-go ahead."

"We will have to talk it over with the rest of my companions," I informed, "but I would be honored and greatly privileged to have the three of you join the team."

Cirdan smiled, "We caught up with the others at the fire last night and they agreed that we should talk to you."

"They were fine with it," Rion blurted.

"You'll still be in charge as I won't be joining," Cirdan added, "Just these two."

"I don't want to be in charge," I groaned, "I don't want anyone to be the leader, I just want us to be a team, a family, making decisions together."

"We come from a pride," Roash explained, "There's an order to things."

"That's what we're used to," Rion breathed in a monotone.

I raised a finger in the air, requesting a short pause and then stuck my head out of my tent, "Balt," I called and then returned my attention back to my guests.

Balt arrived inside my tent as expected, "Wot?"

I pointed at my guests, "These guys."

"Meh, why not?" Balt shrugged and exited my tent.

"We'll figure something out with the whole pride and leadership thing as we go," I said, offering my hand in friendship, "welcome to the team."

Balt suddenly stuck his head back into my tent, "Wot 'r ye gonna do 'bout ta rest o' ta kitties? Are tey all comin' wit us?"

"No," Cirdan quickly answered as he shook my hand, "the rest of us will either stay here on the island, continuing the life we have made here, or go back to our own land and return to the main pride."

"But you have decided to continue on as soldiers?" I asked.

"It's what we're used to," Rion repeated.

"Are you ready to tear this tent down yet? "Oh, we have visitors," Loher called as she blindly walked into the tent.

"Rion and Roash have joined the team," I announced with a smile.

"Surprise," Rion happily moaned.

Balt just laughed and walked away.

"Good, I'm Loher," she spewed, "you can help; we need to get this tent down."

I began to politely usher them out of the tent.

"They will help," Cirdan offered, "their gear is already aboard the Tarantula."

"The Scorpion," Roash quietly corrected in an almost playful manner.

"Okay," Loher acknowledged, "you," she said, beckoning Roash, "follow me, the rest of you, drop this tent."

"No leader," Rion chuckled.

"Please," Loher called back from outside.

"She's normally not like this," I defended as I showed my new companion how to tear down the tent.

⸺◆⸺

The Scorpion looked almost brand new as I loaded the rest of our gear aboard, the only thing she was missing was a fresh coat of paint.

As I walked across the deck, I could hear sailors calling to the people still ashore, "Whoever is coming aboard must get aboard in the next five minutes or else stay ashore. Whoever is aboard and is not going with us, must disembark the ship immediately, or you will be stuck aboard. You have five minutes. Fair Warning."

I began to search for my companions and quickly found them in the mess hall teaching the errfords how to eat a grapefruit.

Nitch and a few of his friends had decided to remain with their chosen buddy.

Mine had apparently chosen to stay on the island, as did Loher's, Kuchoff's, Balt's and Meeka's.

I suddenly realized that our two new eline companions were not present.

"I'm not getting off of the ship, but I have to go look for Rion and Roash." I said as I started for the door.

"They're in the hold," Kuchoff informed as he handed his legendary katana to me, "they're not comfortable being surrounded by so much water and they said that they'd keep an eye on the old wizards."

"I understand," I said as I took the sword, unsheathed it and inspected the blade.

The sword was pristine.

It looked far better than it did when Byron had it.

I handed the sword back to him and said, "Impressive, I'm proud of you."

I was expecting his usual toothy grin, but instead, I got a smile and a firm handshake.

Loher and Meeka gave out an excited breath as we suddenly felt the ship lurch forward as the wind filled her sails and she finally began to move out to sea.

"Tat wand 'ad better work 'r' tis is gonna be a shart trip," Balt stated as he grabbed the edge of the table to steady himself as the ship sharply turned to leave the cove.

"Do you trust me Balt?" Meeka asked.

"O'carse I do," the dwarven warrior immediately answered, "wit me life."

Meeka only smiled and roughly punched him in the arm as she walked past him toward the door, wand in hand.

"She's going to do it soon, you'd better hurry if you want to watch," Kuchoff sang as he followed her out the door, katana securely strapped to his back.

Loher followed soon after, looking back at me to make sure I was following her.

"Let's go, Balt," I laughed as I moved toward the door.

"Bah, magic." Balt grunted with a frown.

I'm not sure if he followed me out.

Once topside, I looked back at the island and saw that we had traveled a great distance in such a short amount of time.

"De wind is in our favor, Mon," Captain Waxx explained as if he had read my mind.

"Are you ready to go back?" I asked.

"As if we neva came," the pirate captain answered.

A bright pink mist suddenly began to envelop The Scorpion.

Red and orange lightning began to web across the sky and the ship began to feel like it was twisting as if caught in a whirlpool.

I looked over to the deck where Meeka was standing in the center of the ship and saw her with the wand high above her head, surrounded by the bright pink mist.

The lightning was emulating from the tip of her wand and creating some sort of vortex or tornado in the mist high above our heads.

The mist began to become thicker and thicker until all we could see was the bright pink with red and orange webs of lightning.

After what seemed like only a few minutes, the pink mist began to dissipate, and the red and orange lightning began to turn back into the normal white and blue.

The Scorpion had stopped twisting and the familiar up and down rocking of waves could be enjoyed once again.

A cheer thundered across the decks as we finally emerged through the mist and found ourselves sailing directly toward Avilyn Harbor.

I chanced a look at Captain Waxx and saw that he had very large tears streaming down his ebony face.

Meeka!

I quickly turned and looked toward where Meeka had been standing and saw her embracing Kuchoff with Balt standing, crying, nearby.

Brother Fost and Nitch were peeking out from the door to the hold, along with our two new eline companions, staring in wonder at the new world that had been presented to them.

The Scorpion sailed past Avilyn Harbor and proceeded toward the river that led to the castle.

My mind began to dwell on Stahvee, my horse, and on my small home just outside the Seolfer Wudu.

Loher gently grasped my arm and whispered in my ear, "We've got a lot of planning to do."

CHAPTER TEN

SUPREMUM ARMORUM SONITUM

As The Scorpion navigated the narrow river, the closer to the castle we ventured, the more we saw villagers taking up arms and begin to run toward the castle.

I looked ahead and saw faint plumes of smoke rising in the distance.

"Can you make this thing go any faster?" I asked the captain and directed his attention to the smoke.

The captain looked up and saw the smoke, "Go and get de boy, Mon," he suggested, "He's done it before..."

I let his words trail off behind me as I ran around and searched for Kuchoff.

I found him in the hold with Roash, Fost and Nitch.

They were teaching him the fundamentals of swordplay.

"Kuchoff," I coughed, "Captain needs you on the bridge."

The young man's eyes lit up, "Psi-Time," I heard him say under his breath as he smiled and headed to the stairs.

He was gone in a flash, and I had a slight problem keeping up with him.

"Reporting as requested, Captain," Kuchoff announced as he reached the bridge.

Without looking up from his journal, the captain calmly pointed in the direction of the smoke.

"Psi-Time," Kuchoff hissed in excitement and left the bridge.

I watched him position himself just below the main sail and close his eyes.

The wind came ever-so-slightly at first, but as the sails began to expand, the wind blew harder and harder until The Scorpion began to skip on the waves that were rushing below her.

I saw the helmsman lose control of the wheel, due to the intense speed, but the ship never went off course.

The landscape was flying past us as we sped toward the castle and whatever was going on there.

As we approached the Island that the castle was built upon, Kuchoff allowed the ship to slow down to its natural momentum and we noticed that the smoke was on the opposite side of the river.

I breathed a sigh of relief that the castle was unharmed but began to worry about the innocent people in whatever town or village was on fire.

Villagers from all around were seen running toward whatever nightmare was happening.

It had to be something big, because we could see the ferry unloading a large unit of Royal Soldiers in full battle gear.

The Royal Soldiers were running further inland toward the smoke.

"This is taking too long," Loher stated as she and Meeka arrived on the bridge.

"As soon as we dock," I informed, "we will go help out."

"Everyone else is teamed up and waiting for us in the hold," Meeka corrected as she and Loher each grabbed one of my hands and led me to the hold.

As soon as we arrived in the hold, we all gathered into a tight circle as the now, bright pink mist surrounded us…

———◦———

…We found ourselves standing a few meters on shore near the path that led inland toward the nightmare that awaited us.

The bright pink mist quickly evaporated and was gone.

"Fun," Rion chuckled.

We quickly began to make our way down the path.

After a few moments of silent travel, I wondered aloud, "Who's watching the wizards?"

"Captain Waxx ordered a few of his men to keep an eye on them for us," Meeka assured.

"They're harmless," Roash laughed, "Relax."

"Famous last words," Balt chuckled.

Rion let out a snort.

We walked on for a while, keeping an eye on the smoke as we grew closer.

The smoke never changed color or volume, so we didn't really know what to make of it.

Occasionally, we would encounter a Royal Soldier or two heading back to the harbor, looking worse for wear.

We tried to speak to them, but they were too intent on getting away from whatever waited ahead.

The closer we walked toward the fighting, the more often we would find villagers and Royal Soldiers either dead from their injuries or dying and unable to speak.

Small fires were smoldering or still burning on as we could finally hear men screaming and weapons clashing.

Then, we finally saw the corpse of a Magara.

The magara were a race of sub-human barbarians that dwelled in the hills near the base of the Ferrum Mons.

Warlike and criminal, it was rare to encounter them, but if you did, it meant mass hysteria and total destruction.

Balt identified and informed us of our soon-to-be-rivals and jovially picked up the pace.

Our eline companions followed suit and began to quietly emit a purr-like hum.

Picking up on the excitement, Kuchoff drew his katana and rushed ahead to catch up with Balt.

"Bows?" Loher asked.

"Bows," I agreed and began to string up my bow.

Meeka and Fost began to quietly chant and all suddenly felt right in the world.

The stench of burning flesh permeated the air as we strategically entered the battlefield.

Bodies of humans and magara littered the paths that led from hut to hut in this once quaint little village.

Huts and shoppes were burning to the ground as frightened villagers rushed around trying to extinguish the flames without being cut down by the ever-present enemy.

"It's guid ta be 'ome!" Balt laughed as he cut the legs out from under one of the cavemen.

I just snorted out a laugh as I pulled my Invisibility Cloak's hood over my head and notched an arrow to my bowstring.

Loher followed suit and began to peg off the enemy with deadly accurate headshots.

Kuchoff was doing exceptionally well, considering he wasn't tripping all over bodies yet as he neutralized four magara without even moving his feet from where they were planted.

A barrage of well-aimed energy balls suddenly buzzed over our heads as Meeka let loose on our foes.

Magara began to scatter from the new magical bursts as several of them suddenly just dropped where they stood.

Sudden roars let loose to our right as we witnessed Rion perform his apparently famous stampede maneuver.

Somehow, he managed to tuck his enormous hulk of a body behind the mid-sized shield he carried and proceeded to run headlong into a substantially sized group of equally proportioned magara.

Rion drew his sword at the last moment before impact.

A loud crash of flesh and bone ensued as the two large masses collided, sending the cut up and mangled bodies of the enemy flying in all directions.

Loher suddenly laughed and pointed my attention to what at first seemed like nothing until I saw a magara fall for no apparent reason, then another and another.

I had to take a closer look to see the vague form of Roash, lurking in the shadows and smoke, slashing the throats of her victims, silently, as if she wasn't even there.

Rion, on the other hand, had somehow, quickly made his way near Kuchoff and Balt and was trying to begin a friendly competition between the three to see who could kill the fastest, or cleanest, or bloodiest; the list went on.

Fost and Nitch seemed almost happy as they dodged in and out of hiding places, healing the wounded villagers as they found them.

Fost would fire off a few bolts from his Blessed Crossbow if the need presented itself, but for the most part, they would hide and heal.

Although the magara outnumbered my team approximately seven to one, not including the villagers, victory was ours and the long and emotional aftermath of war had begun for the villagers.

Praise and thanks for our help was neither needed nor wanted, so my team and I had decided to take advantage of the smoke and make our exit back to the harbor area as quickly and as quietly as we could.

The trek back to The Scorpion, which was waiting for us at the docks, didn't seem as long, although Brother Fost and Nitch wanted to stop and examine each and every wounded soldier we encountered.

Finally, back aboard The Scorpion, we set our course back to the South Harbor on the island and set sail.

Chapter Eleven

BEATITUDE

As soon as we entered the gates of Salvus Hus, Loher and I proceeded to the stables and Festus to check on our horses, Stahvee and Amaryllis.

Our companions informed us that they would be in 'The Broken Blade' for a meal and a few well-deserved drinks.

"Welcome back, weary adventurers," Festus greeted as we entered the stables.

"You wouldn't believe what we've been through," I breathed as I stroked the head and ears of my loyal steed.

"I figured you'd make it back sooner or later," a familiar tiny voice announced from behind me, "You all were gone already by the time I returned."

"Brendt," I recognized and turned around.

"It's probably a good thing you were already gone," he said as he flitted around and finally came to a rest on Stahvee's head, which annoyed the horse who in turn proceeded to shake him off.

Why's that?" Loher asked.

Brendt landed gently on my shoulder and told us, "Sadly, I couldn't find a solution to your problem," he admitted, "but you're here now and that's all that matters."

"What do we owe you, Festus?" I asked as my stomach growled loudly enough for him to hear.

"We'll take care of that later," the old stableman announced with a wave of his hand, "go on now, to 'The Broken Blade' and have a meal. I can hear your stomach tattling on you."

"Thank you, Festus, we'll be back in the morning, if that's alright," Loher suggested as Brendt took flight away from my shoulder and flitted around the room.

"That would be fine, my dear," Festus laughed and politely ushered us to the door, "Please tell Sir Quinn that his horse is here as well. She just wandered back in here as if she knew where to go."

The smile on the old man's face suddenly dropped as he realized from the looks on our own that the knight had not made it.

"My condolences," Festus said in a low voice as he removed his hat and hung his head, "was it quick at least?"

"In a flash," I solemnly answered and exited the building.

———◆———

The festivities were already in full swing as Loher, Brendt and I entered the darkened tavern.

Our eyes had to adjust to the change from bright sunlight to sudden darkness before we could proceed into the room.

At our usual table, Balt was toasting the team with a round of drinks while our eline companions nervously looked around at the other patrons.

The two other patrons were a human male and female pair of apparent nobility and probably didn't know the difference between an orc and a hobgoblin, let alone what an eline is, although the differences were hugely obvious.

Sufficed to say, they weren't paying any attention to anything but themselves, and rightly so.

"You can relax," I said to the pair of eline as Loher and I took our seats, "no one is going to harm you in this realm."

"Not no one 'ere in tis tavern anyways," Balt laughed and poured another round of drinks.

"I suppose it is silly," Roash admitted.

"Not really," Brother Fost studiously added, "considering you're all from a different realm, it will most likely take some time before any of you are fully comfortable here."

"That includes me too," Nitch added from somewhere inside Fost's hood.

"We're not used to it yet," Rion moaned.

"A man o' a t'ousand words," Balt quipped.

"Balt," Loher scolded, "that's not nice."

"Wot?" Balt asked in defense, "Tat's all I heared from 'im so far. About a t'ousand words."

"I don't talk good," Rion half moaned, and half giggled.

"But ye kin fight good, and tat's all tat matters ta me, Mate," the dwarf said and slapped Rion on the back playfully.

"I fight good," Rion echoed with a bright smile.

"Aye, Mate, ye do," Balt said as he raised his mug.

"Somebody has a wedding to plan!" Brendt sang, reminding everyone excitedly.

"Shut up, Brendt," Loher and I hissed.

"Did I just hear something about planning a wedding?" A young, familiar voice asked from the doorway.

We turned to look at the door and found none other than King Lagu Ofer 'Eal.

"Your Highness!" We all (except the eline) sang in reverence.

The King shook his head with a slight smile and a wave of his hand, "I detest such formality."

"What can I offer you, my Liege?" The new barkeep asked as the King took up a seat at our table.

"Do you have any milk?" The King asked.

"Goat or cow?"

"Cow, please."

"Right away."

"I've always wanted to perform a wedding ceremony," the King directed toward us, "the castle grounds are beautiful, and the weather is perfect! Who's getting married?"

As if it were planned, Brendt took flight from the table, magically produced two small bells and proceeded to ring them over the heads of Loher and myself.

"The Lovebirds, my Liege," Brendt sang as we attempted to swat him away like an annoying fly.

Annoying is the key word.

"What have you planned so far?" The King asked with full interest.

Loher and I looked at each other with confusion, horror and extreme embarrassment dripping from our faces, panicking.

"They've only *just* gotten engaged, your Highness," Meeka explained, soothing some anxiety.

"Then I've caught you at the right time," the King smiled.

"I want to get married on The Scorpion," Loher suddenly blurted out.

"Ahh yes, The Scorpion," the young King breathed, "I'd like to see this ship, perhaps you could take me there?"

"At your convenience, your Highness," I agreed.

"No better time than the present," he said as he finished his milk, leaving a white milk moustache behind, "Finish your meals, I'll be right back with one of my guards."

As soon as the King left the tavern, I turned to Loher, "On The Scorpion?"

"Yeah, why not?" She asked.

"No offence to anyone, but I can barely understand Captain Waxx's accent." I admitted.

"Me neit'er." Balt added.

Brother Fost loudly cleared his throat with a pained look on his face, "In case you didn't know," the priest began, "I too, can perform wedding ceremonies."

"Do you want to do it, Brother Fost?" Loher asked in an apologetic voice.

"Onh, no!" Brother Fost laughed, holding his rotund belly, "I'm excited to hear Captain Waxx do it!"

"What does Captain Waxx's accent have to do with getting married on The Scorpion?" Kuchoff asked.

"The captain of a ship is allowed to preform ceremonies if aboard the ship," I began, "if Captain Waxx preforms the ceremony, we won't be able to understand it very well, therefore, we won't enjoy it as much."

"The King seems keen on performing the ceremony," Kuchoff advised.

"That's something the captain and the King will have to discuss." I stated.

"Meeka, my dear, will you do us the honor?" The King asked as he and an armored bodyguard entered the tavern.

"The what?" She asked, surprised and confused, "I'm sorry, your Highness, but I..." Meeka shyly began.

The King, smiling from ear to ear like an excited child, (which he wasn't anymore,) began to pantomime circling smoke and mist with his hands and arms, "Poof, the mist, the smoke, the smoke..."

Meeka smiled, closed her eyes, and raised her hands.

***

The pink mist quickly evaporated, and we found ourselves standing a few meters away from the boarding dock to The Scorpion.

The sailors were just putting the finishing touches of paint on The Scorpion's coat, and she looked shiny and brand new.

'The best I've ever seen her look,' I thought to myself.

"Oi, Mate!" Balt called out as he found Captain Waxx.

"Oi, Mon." The captain called down.

"Permissions ta come aboard, Cap'n?" Balt called up, splaying his hand toward the rest of us.

"Who are dey?" Waxx asked, pointing at the King and his guard.

"Ta King an 'is guard," Balt half shouted, half hissed, trying to keep the King and his guard a secret.

"Granted, bruddahs an sistahs," The captain joyfully called down.

We all shuffled to the gangplank and one-by-one, filed aboard the ship.

Unable to see well in his helmet, the King's guard lost his footing and began to fall off the plank, and into the water, but with quick (cat-like) reflexes and powerful strength, Rion caught him before he fell too far.

Like the proverbial bride and groom, Rion carried the guard over the railing of the ship and gently set him down on the deck.

The King was visibly overjoyed.

"My thanks to you," the guard offered as he pulled off his helmet.

He was only around seventeen years old, very young, but physically built like a musclebound grown man.

"Friends," Rion moaned back.

The guard gave the eline warrior a worried look and then suddenly jumped...

"Lemme see tat," Balt spat as he grabbed the guard's helmet, startling him.

The dwarf examined the guard's helmet for a few seconds, pulled a tool from his belt, tapped, bent and pulled at something, spat on it to shine it up and handed it back, "Put it on," Balt growled.

The guard nervously complied.

"Look around, Boy-o," Balt jeered, "walk around an' see if ye c'n see any better."

The guard turned his head back and forth, up and down, and then walked a few paces.

He pantomimed drawing his sword and fighting an invisible enemy, flailing around like a mad man.

Kuchoff and the King began to giggle.

"Wow! This is incredible, what did you do to fix it?" The guard asked.

"I didn't fix it, Mate," Balt laughed, "I made it better."

"My thanks to you as well," said the Guard with a grin.

"Now lemme see tat sward." Balt reached.

The guard's grin disappeared as he quickly blocked the dwarf's reach and turned to the King.

The King was laughing along with Kuchoff and Meeka.

"Now dat de games is over, Mon, where we goin'?" Captain Waxx asked with a chuckle.

"No where, right now," I answered.

"Den why-?" he began.

"It's a long story, besides," I paused and looked around, "the King wants a tour of your boat."

"She's not a boat, Mon," the captain said angrily and stomped his foot, "she's a ship. Big difference."

"My apologies," I stated, slowly backing away with splayed hands, "she's a ship, she's a ship."

"Boats don't have sails," he spat and returned to the bridge, still cursing me until he slammed the door.

'Boats don't have sails, got it.' I said to myself as I joined the rest of my team.

"What was that, Love?" Loher asked as I walked up.

"Boats don't have sails."

She cringed, "You didn't."

I nodded my head in shame.

"You *should* be ashamed," she giggled and kissed my cheek, "come on, we have a tour to go on."

⚬

The tour seemed to last forever as the King had many, many questions.

But somewhere between the beginning and the end of the tour, the King had somehow convinced the captain to let him perform the wedding ceremony aboard The Scorpion.

"Really?" I asked, "you just gave in with no arguments?"

"Ja, Mon," Waxx laughed, "'e kin do it all 'e wants, Mon, 'e's de King."

"Here on The Scorpion?"

"Right 'ere on De Scorpion, Mon, I don't mind at'tall."

"Thanks, Mario, you're a true friend."

"No I ain't," he said with a sly grin as he looked down at a map.

"You're not still angry with me for my earlier choice of words, are you?"

The captain just sighed, never looking up from the map, silently dismissing me from the bridge.

As I exited the bridge, a sailor caught up with me, "We built you each sleeping quarters below, in case you're interested."

"Incredible!" I gasped, "Thank you," I paused, "What happened to the three wizards we had in the brig?

"Nobody told you?" The sailor blinked.

I shook my head as a negative.

The sailor shyly smiled and conceded, "Somehow, they escaped in the preparation for your wedding."

Before I could respond, he was swiftly jogging away to perform other duties.

It was getting late, and I had, some moments ago, seen the puff of pink smoke when Meeka blinked the King and his guard back to the castle, so I decided to go below to secure sleeping quarters.

Loher was already down there and had already picked out suitable quarters for us, right next door to Meeka and Roash.

Kuchoff decided to bunk in with Brother Fost and Nitch, while Balt and Rion took the room near the stairs.

We all retired for the night.

"Did you know that the three wizards escaped?" I asked Loher as I entered the room.

"Dammit." Loher cursed. "I knew there was something I was forgetting to tell you, but with the wedd—"

"I understand," I soothed, "we've all been excited and busy."

I sat on the bed and pulled my boots off.

"A squad of sailors are out looking for them as we speak," she assured, "the local authorities as well as the King's men have been informed; they won't get very far."

"Unless they somehow 'magicked' themselves back to whatever rock they crawled out from under."

"Well," Loher half frowned, "there *is* that."

"After the wedding," I stated, "I think we should go after them."

"How?" She asked, "Where?"

I laughed, "I don't know, but we'll figure it out."

"Perhaps word on the street will help," Loher added, "Three guys in purple robes couldn't have gone unnoticed by everyone. Someone has *had to* have seen something."

"It's late," I yawned, "I'm exhausted."

"I'll let you sleep," Loher cooed and kissed my forehead.

I drifted off into dreamland with the thoughts of marrying Loher on my mind.

⚬

Besides Loher, who didn't need to sleep very often, I was the first of our team to rise.

Loher greeted me, once again, with a welcomed cup of coffee, "You know," I yawned, "as much as I appreciate this," I raised the mug, "you don't..."

Loher cut me off, "I enjoy it."

"Exactly what part of doing things for me do you enjoy?" I asked.

"Your smile and appreciation," she answered, "believe me, if you didn't appreciate it, I wouldn't do it."

"Fair enough," I admitted and then asked, "do I do enough for you?"

She only smiled and nodded her head as she breathed in the sea air and stared off into the distance.

The sun was resting gently on her face as the wind was lazily blowing her hair into golden waves and curls.

"I think Captain Waxx is still angry with me," I smirked.

"For calling The Scorpion a boat?" Loher chuckled.

My confirmation was drowned out by an eruption of dwarven laughter, "You called Ta Scorpion a **boat**?" Balt chortled, "I ain't surprised tat 'e be cross wit'cha, Mate." Balt sauntered away, still laughing, "'E called Ta Scorpion a boat!"

"What was that all about?" Roash asked as she and Rion strolled into view.

Loher rolled her eyes and laughed, "the boys are just having a go at each other," she smiled, "nothing to worry about. I'm sure it will clear up eventually."

"You know, Meeka snores." Roash stated as a fact.

"I'm sorry," Loher apologized, "I should have warned you."

"It was actually quite comforting," Roash clarified, "My own mother used to purr in her sleep that loud."

"I like that!" Meeka sang as she climbed the stairs, "Did you hear that Kuchoff?" The wizard smiled, "I don't snore, I purr."

Kuchoff laughed and began to exaggerate a snoring, purring sound.

"Brat," Meeka laughed and feigned a swat to his bum but missed on purpose.

Kuchoff smiled and ducked away to find Balt.

"He's not really your son, is he?" Roash guessed.

"He's not," Meeka conceded, "how did you know?"

"Honestly, it was just a... feeling." Roash admitted, "It really doesn't matter to me either way."

"Does he know?" Rion asked innocently.

"Yes, Rion," Meeka blinked, "Kuchoff is well aware that he is not really my son."

"Okay," Rion commented and slowly strolled off to find Balt and Kuchoff.

Moments later, a loud crash could be heard from the direction of the mess hall, followed by an uproar of laughter.

Then, silence.

Loher, Meeka and Roash just looked at each other and shook their heads.

"I'm almost afraid to ask what that might have been." Roash quipped.

We quickly strode to the mess hall, and as we arrived, we saw a few onions, half carrots, chunks of potatoes and...

...Another half of an onion came sailing through the door, followed by another wave of laughter.

"Try an' keep yer eye on t'is one," I heard Balt say through the doorway, "cause I'mma gonna give it full berries."

Curious, I carefully peeked my head in to see what was going on.

Kuchoff was standing near the doorway, his back to me, wielding his katana, while Balt, Rion, the cook, and a few sailors were lobbing vegetables at him.

Balt wound up his pitch and rocketed a large potato at the young man.

The potato missile sped toward Kuchoff faster than I could keep my eyes on it, but Kuchoff swung the blade and cleanly cut the potato in two.

One half landed a few centimeters from my foot.

"What are you guys doing?" Loher half laughed.

"Multi-tasking, Ma'am," the cook answered with no hesitation.

"They're trying to train me to fight with this sword," Kuchoff proudly stated, as he showed off his katana.

"Trying?" a sailor rhetorically asked.

"Oi!" Balt spat, "T'at's na a sward, Boy-o." he winked at me and continued at Kuchoff, "T'at's a katana. Big difference."

"What's the difference, Balt?" I asked, expecting him to not know the real reason.

"Draw yer sward," the dwarf coaxed.

I drew my own blade and handed it to Balt.

Kuchoff handed the katana to him as well.

Balt put the two weapons side to side and compared the length, "Katana's longer," he said and then showed off the actual blades of both, "Katana's blade is t'icker."

Balt walked over to the pile of firewood and picked out two large pieces of comparable size, weight and thickness.

He handed them to me and said, "T'row 'em at me, one at a time."

I waited for him to be ready and then lobbed the first piece.

It sailed through the air, and at the right time, the dwarven warrior swung my sword and made contact.

There was a loud thud as the blade of my sword became lodged in the wood and then fell to the ground due to the unbalanced weight.

It took Balt a moment to dislodge the blade, "Juss wait," he grunted and pulled with all of his mighty dwarven might.

The chunk of wood went sailing one way, while Balt and my sword went the other, landing in each respective corner with a loud crash.

Rion and I began laughing as the dwarf recovered himself.

Brother Fost rushed to the dwarf's side and immediately began to administer any needed healing.

"He's fine," the halfling priest giggled in relief, remembering the sight of Balt going ass over teakettle into the corner.

The rest were either laughing, or trying not to, once Balt was assured to be unharmed.

My blade was free and returned no worse for wear.

"T'row ta ut'er one," he said as he readied the katana.

"Are you sure?" I asked, "Last time—"

"T'row it," Balt growled, "an' give it some berries."

I tossed the second piece exactly how I threw the first, and it too, sailed through the air toward the dwarf.

He swung the katana just the same as he swung my sword and made contact.

Two equal halves dropped to the floor as Balt smiled and took a step back.

"A katana is na a sward," Balt repeated and handed it back to Kuchoff.

As Kuchoff was inspecting the blade, someone lobbed another potato at him.

It looked as if he didn't even think about it as he raised the katana and cut the potato in two.

One half landed by Balt's foot and the other smacked Kuchoff in the face.

"Ow!" Kuchoff croaked.

"T'at's when yer suppost'a deflect," Balt laughed, "whenever it be comin' at yer face."

An apple was thrown.

Then another, and another.

I joined in and began trying to pelt the teenager with fruits and vegetables.

After a short, very short while, the projectiles being thrown at him were either cut to pieces or deflected away from him by a protective personal Psi shield.

"Awe," Balt groaned, "T'at's na fair."

"But it's effective," Kuchoff laughed in pride.

"Ye gots a guid point t'ere, Kid."

Captain Waxx suddenly entered the mess hall and took a look at the mess, "I'll not even be askin' Mon," he said with a pained look on his face, "I'll just be getting me coffee an' pretend dat I didn't see anythn'."

"Well," Balt began, "It **is** ta mess hall."

"Balt!" Roash hissed.

"Wot?" Balt asked, "Ain't it?"

Captain Waxx began to smile and then laugh.

"He reached over and slugged the dwarf on the shoulder, "I like you, Dwarf."

"This wedding isn't going to plan itself now, is it?" Brendt sang as he suddenly appeared in the mess hall.

We were cleaning up the mess from Kuchoff's katana training, when the sprite and a few fairies began to flutter into the room.

"For once, Brendt," Loher stated, "I'm actually happy to see you."

"Touching." Brendt breathed and flitted around her head and shoulders.

"Not **that** happy though," she spewed as she waved her arms and hands around, trying to shoo the sprite away.

He finally came to rest on the back of one of the unoccupied chairs, "So, what have we planned so far? Please don't say, 'nothing.'"

"She wants to get married here, on The Scorpion." I offered.

"Is the captain…" Brendt began with a sour look on his face.

The captain laughed, "No, Mon," Waxx answered, "De King will be doin' de ceremony."

"Well, this is sounding perfect!" Brendt exclaimed, "Are we docking here, or somewhere else?"

"Hmm," Loher thought for a moment, "that's a really good question."

"We should do it somewhere scenic," Meeka cooed, "with flowers and…" She stopped herself, embarrassed, "…I'm sorry," she confessed, "you guys should really be the ones to decide."

"Your suggestions are always welcome, Meeka," Loher assured.

"I know of a place," Balt said, softly.

"Romantic tips from a dwarf," Brother Fost giggled, "this should be good."

"Let's hear him out," I playfully scolded.

Balt stuck his tongue out at the priest, making Kuchoff, Rion and me laugh, "T'ere's a place off the coast of the Ferrum Mons tat we used ta take our wimmins ta court 'em."

"Desolate and rocky doesn't really sound like the perfect place," Brother Fost jeered.

"Can you show us, Balt?" Loher asked.

"We shuld go an git ta King b'fore we sail all ta way out t'ere," Balt warned, "cuz yor gonna wanna git married right away whens ya see ta place."

Brother Fost just smiled and obnoxiously rolled his eyes at his friend, the dwarf.

"Ye'll see, Priest," Balt laughed, playing along, "ye'll see."

"We should go into town and pick up some needed things," Loher suggested.

"Like rings, and a dress?" Meeka excitedly asked.

"Among other things," Loher answered with a smile.

"I already have your ring," I smiled at Loher.

"Can I go with you?" Kuchoff asked as he tugged at his shirt, "I'm outgrowing my clothes."

"I was about ta say sompt'in' 'bout t'at, Kid," Balt added, "I noticed t'at when ye would try an' block high shots, ye was 'avin' a bit o' troubles."

Kuchoff vigorously nodded his head, agreeing.

"Anyone else?" Loher asked the room.

"Is it safe if I go?" Roash shyly asked.

"Of course," Meeka soothed, "why wouldn't it be?"

Roash only looked around as if in a panic.

"She is only one of two eline in this realm," Brother Fost answered instead.

Roash shyly agreed with a smile and a nod.

"You'll be perfectly safe, Roash," Loher added, "I'm sure no one will even give you a third look."

"Third look?" Roash asked, a bit more at ease.

"Well, I'm sure you'll turn a few heads of curiosity, and make others do a simple double-take," Loher chuckled and put her arm around the female eline's shoulder as the three women began to leave the room.

Kuchoff stood up, tossed his handful of debris into the bin and followed the women out.

"You didn't want to go, Thunor?" Brother Fost asked as he wiped the last of the mess off the table and into the bin.

I shook my head, no and pushed a few chairs into their designated places, "I have to pick out the perfect ring from my stash."

"You have a stash of rings?" The priest asked.

I looked at the pint-sized adventurer in shock, "You don't?"

"I'm a priest," Brother Fost smiled, "I have no need for rings and trinkets."

I smiled in understanding.

The halfling priest picked up an unmolested apple, smiled at me and took a bite as he exited the room.

I took a quick look around at the now clean mess hall, smiled and sighed a satisfied sigh, and then headed for my quarters to find that one, perfect, ring.

As I exited the mess hall, Meeka's pink smoke, from blinking herself, Loher, Roash and Kuchoff to town, was fading away.

I made my way down to my quarters and located my stash of treasures.

Music could be heard from the hold, as a group of sailors practiced a few jaunty tunes on various instruments.

My stash box was full of diverse treasures that I thought would come in handy, further down the road.

It turns out, I was right.

I shuffled through the box until I picked out two rings that I thought would serve the purpose.

"Hey, Balt," I called out my door.

"Wot did I do now?" Balt grumbled as he poked his head into my doorway.

"Which of these two rings..." I began.

"T'is one!" Balt exclaimed, as he snatched the ring from my hand and began to study it.

A smile: the biggest smile I have ever seen the dwarf wear, suddenly washed over his face.

He honestly wiped a tear from his eye as he handed the ring back to me with care.

He pointed to the ring, never taking his eyes from it and explained, "I mined t'ose jewels," he blinked and then looked me in the eye, "I crafted t'at ring, where'd ye obtain it?"

"One of the wizards I captured was wearing it," I answered.

"An' t'ey escaped," Balt frowned, "I'd like ta 'ave been able ta question 'im."

"It won't be easy," I admitted, "but we'll find them."

"T'unor," Balt said with all seriousness and put his hand on my shoulder, "it would be an honor if you gave t'at ring ta Loher as her wedding ring."

"Balt," I sniffed as tears welled up in my eyes, "the honor would be ours," I paused, "Loher's and mine."

"T'en it be settled," Balt laughed and slugged me hard in the arm, "t'at be t'e ring."

<hr>

A huge puff of pink smoke suddenly filled the hallway between personal quarters, accompanied by the familiar 'pop' as two golden armored knights stepped out, followed by a veiled figure adorned in a long, flowing white dress.

Soon after, a man dressed in full leather armor, the color of rich reddish brown, with tall black boots appeared.

It wasn't until Roash, Meeka and then finally, the King and two more golden guards stepped out and the pink smoke dissipated that I realized who everyone was.

"I have never seen such **beauty**!" I involuntarily exclaimed as Loher raised her veil.

"Thanks!" Kuchoff laughed, knowing I was talking about Loher, "It's a little big, but Roash says I'll grow into it soon."

Loher just stood there, glowing, with a shy yet beautiful smile.

Brother Fost suddenly burst from his quarters and grabbed Loher, pulling her into our quarters, "Its bad luck to see the bride before the wedding!"

They disappeared into my room and slammed the door, "Go away, Thunor," the priest yelled from behind the door.

"Yer new armor looks guid, Mate," Balt chuckled and roughly turned the teenager around to get a good look.

"How's it feel?" I asked, also admiring the kid's new look.

"It's a little stiff, but the guild master said it would be until, I break it in."

"It helps to wear padding under it for a while," I offered, "until it softens up."

"I am," Kuchoff smiled, and pulled on a bit of the padding to show me.

Chapter Twelve

NOCES

The young King was enjoying his first voyage aboard The Scorpion, and as we rounded the bend from the river, past Avilyn Harbor, the King shared with us that this was the furthest away from the castle that he had ever been.

He also admitted that he had never been on a ship (or boat) before and that he was initially worried about what it would be like, but he was having fun, so all was well in his world.

We had been on the water for about three hours before either one of our eline companions decided to brave the upper decks.

"'ow kin such a deadly warrior be afraid o' such a simple ting as sea travel?" Balt rhetorically asked as Rion poked his head up from the stairway to the hold.

Rion only looked around nervously and didn't answer.

Roash scoffed and shot the dwarf a stern look, "It takes him a little while to get used to change," she advised, "he'll come out eventually."

"Ahh," Balt coughed, "I'm only funnin' 'im."

"We're coming up on the Ferrum Mons, Balt," I announced as I walked up to the trio of fighters, "you might want to head to the bridge and inform the captain of our next moves."

"Aye, Mate," Balt said with a quick snap of his meaty fingers, "I be on it."

"Don't worry, Rion," Roash soothed as Balt turned the corner on his way to the bridge, "We'll be there soon."

"He's still a bit scared of the motion?" I asked.

"Yeah," Roash sighed, "he'll be just fine as soon as we stop moving."

"Well, according to Balt, we should be almost there." I offered.

"Balt seems trustworthy," Roash smiled, "and I'm sure the location will be exactly what your bride wanted."

"I've grown quite fond of the dwarf." I admitted, and then suddenly realized that my statement was true. I actually did love the rude little nut ball.

I have grown attached to everyone on the team.

I missed Sir Quinn and Byron.

Orders began to be called out and sailors were running around, lowering sails and dropping anchors.

We could feel The Scorpion begin to slow to a stop and Rion seemed to gain his confidence back.

My team and I gathered at the front of the ship to take a good look around.

Brother Fost was only half correct, because nestled into the desolate rocky drabness, we spotted a lush, beautiful, color infused tropical paradise that only spanned a few dozen meters along the shoreline.

"Wow!" The young King gasped, "This is in my realm?"

"Aye, M'lord," Balt beamed, "been 'ere fer as long as I c'n ramember."

"This spot is perfect, Balt!" Loher cried and threw her arms around him in an awkward embrace.

Balt stood there not knowing how to take the sudden affection, so he just sighed and allowed it to happen.

Meeka was glowing with delight, with a Kuchoff-like toothy grin plastered upon her face.

Speaking of Kuchoff, "Has anyone seen Kuchoff?" I asked, looking around.

Everyone spread out and began looking for him...

"There he is!" Meeka breathed in awe.

On the beach, Kuchoff and Captain Waxx, were gathering flowers and making ornate arrangements.

"I thought we were getting married **on** The Scorpion," I whispered in Loher's ear.

"We are, Silly," she whispered back and pointed to the ship's bridge.

It turns out, while we were gazing at the beautiful surroundings, the crew of The Scorpion and Kuchoff were setting up an area near the bridge with flowers and succulents they had already gathered from around the castle grounds.

All they needed were the finishing touches from the beach we had arrived at.

"Captain Waxx and his crew put this all together," Loher smiled, "I'm sure he's not angry with you anymore; he just couldn't let out the secret."

Everyone aboard assembled near The Scorpion's bridge in a sort of semicircle around a makeshift stage.

King Lagu Ofer 'Eal was standing in the center of the stage while I stood before him.

The stage and the surrounding areas were decorated quite colorfully, as dozens of honeybees, butterflies and fairies flittered about, enhancing the beauty and charm.

The beautiful, color-filled tropical shoreline nestled into the drab, gray, rocky dreariness was an awesome spectacle of a backdrop for the scene.

The weather was nice, and the wind was just barely a breeze.

Birds of all species were singing songs of their kind, creating a sort of symphonic soundtrack for the proceedings.

Kuchoff, Brother Fost and a handful of sailors began to softly play a slow tune on their various instruments, as Loher was escorted down our makeshift aisle by two of the King's guards.

Her dress flowed behind her like waves of blowing snow, and the contrast between the golden armor of the Royal guards and her dress set off a vibrant shimmer, increasing her already natural glow.

She smiled at me as the guards ushered her to my side.

We stood nervously before the teenaged King.

The King looked equally as nervous as he looked around at the three hundred or so individuals in the audience.

The music slowly faded to a stop.

The young King cleared his throat and began: "Dearly Beloved, we are gathered here, this day, in front of Onh and this company, to witness and celebrate one of this life's greatest moments; to give recognition to the worth and beauty of love, and to add our best wishes and blessings to the union of Loher, daughter of D'Rolwynn and Thunor, son of McLaaud."

Captain Waxx stepped forward, cleared his throat and began, "De first time you came aboard me **ship**, De Scorpion, I saw de spark between de pair of you in me eyes.

Over d'ese last sev'ral years, I was honored to see two advent'erers such as yorselves gettin' closer.

De way you both work toget'er with very little talking is as if yo're mind readin' de other.

It's almost like de wild magic d'at Meeka conjures.

Maybe d'at's how elves be, but you seem closer d'an any I've met.

Most captains would regale you wit sea stories o' grand adventure, but since we've been on some of de best adventures toget'er, d'at seems trite.

Instead, I wrote somet'ing special for you.

True friendship is rare in d'ese perilous times.

Sometimes our journey crosses wit others, and if yo're truly lucky, d'ey become true friends.

Yor entire team is an amazing example of true friendship.

All romantic relationships start in friendship.

T'unor and Loher, your friendship grew 'til t'was obvious you had found de missing pieces of yor souls.

You've saved each ut'er's lives countless times, so yor lives honestly belong to de ut'er.

Even being undead or being stranded on an island could not sully yor relationship.

Me?

I' be a pirate.

De Scorpion be me beloved, the sea be me mistress and me crew be me family.

D'at be 'nough for a pirate.

Likewise, you 'ave found each ut'er and de rest of yor team has become family.

I wish you many more adventures, love, happiness and lots of treasure!

And if you ever need it transported and want to share (wink), De Scorpion would be happy to help.

Now let's get on wit dis joyous occasion!" Cap'n Waxx let out a hearty laugh.

The King continued, "Loher and Thunor, marriage is an institution ordained by Onh, and is not to be entered into lightly or unadvisedly, but reverently, deliberately, and after much consideration, for, in coming together in marriage, you are committing yourselves exclusively, the one to the other, for all of eternity."

He paused for effect and then continued, "Knowing this, I ask of you this question:

Do you, Thunor, choose Loher on this day; to speak the words that will join you with her, as your wife, for all of eternity? If so, please answer, 'I do.'"

"I do," Thunor smiled and looked at Loher.

"Do you, Loher, choose Thunor on this day; to speak the words that will join you with him as your husband, for all of eternity? If so, please answer, 'I do.'"

"I do," Loher beamed.

The King smiled and continued, "If you would please turn to face one another and join hands as you each speak your marital vows."

Loher blushed, took a deep breath and began: "Thunor, I remember the first time you told me that I was beautiful – how sincere you were and how incredulous I was that I didn't see it.

The truth is, My Love, that it is you that makes me feel beautiful.

You were that missing piece in my life, and it changed everything.

When I decided to follow you to that cave, I took a leap of faith that I have never regretted; I've never looked back.

I dared you to take me on an adventure and you have done that and so much more.

I want to wake up to you each morning and end the day with you each night.

I want to know, beyond the shadow of a doubt, that my best friend will be right there beside me – through every smile and every tear; through frustrations and anguish, and joy and elation; providing comfort when I'm sick and a gut check when I need one.

And I promise you that I will always be with you – always support you – always comfort you.

I will do my best to always make you happy, apologize when I'm wrong, and keep you grounded.

There has never been anyone this special in my heart; someone so amazing, brilliant, funny, creative and loving.

So, My Love, no matter if I'm angry or sad, frustrated or excited, content, peaceful or happy; I promise, from the bottom of my soul, that I will always love you – beyond this life – without end."

I looked at our companions standing around us and I think I can safely say that there was barely a dry eye on deck.

Balt was even pretending that he had something in his eye.

It was my turn now.

"Loher, My Love," I nervously and excitedly began, "words cannot describe the feelings I am experiencing for you.

It is just so easy for me to tell you that I love you, but the words for the feelings I am honestly feeling for you get lost somewhere in translation, so, I promise to show you exactly how I feel; you **will** know love.

You will understand what love really is and how it is supposed to feel.

I cannot wait to hold you in my arms from this day forward and allow you to know that you are safe and loved.

You'll enjoy the feelings that you deserve to feel and have been missing out on for so long.

When you wandered into my life, you literally moved my soul.

I'm always here, in all ways, especially when life gets difficult.

You are only one single person in this world, but to **this** one single person, you **are** the world.

A piece of you has grown inside of me, so in essence, My Love, you see, it's you and me together, forever.

My heart is full of so many feelings to say to you, and there are moments when I feel that simple words amount to nothing at all.

Be happy.

Be my true, my only, my all as I am.

Always only yours."

I looked up and caught the King wiping tears from his eyes, "What tokens of love and respect do you offer each other?"

Captain Waxx stepped forward and handed out two golden rings.

The King continued, "The wedding ring is the outward sign of an inward and spiritual grace, signifying to all, the union of this man, and this woman, in holy matrimony.

I believe it was the wise old bard, Augustine, who said, 'The nature of Onh is like a circle whose center is everywhere and circumference is nowhere.'

May the rings that you hold symbolize the nature of Onh in your lives, and as often as either of you see them, may you be reminded of this very moment and the endless love that you have promised."

I thought I could hear Balt snoring, so I took a quick look back at the audience and saw that it was actually Nitch in Brother Fost's hood.

The priest quickly nudged Nitch enough to quiet him down, and the wedding continued.

"Thunor," the King initiated, "as you present Loher with her wedding ring, and pledge your love and life to her, will you please repeat after me:

Loher, I give you this ring as a symbol of my love...

With all that I am and all that I have...

I promise to love and honor you, always.

With this ring, I thee wed."

I think I could actually **hear** Balt smile with pride as I showed Loher the ring.

Loher noticed the dwarf's beaming smile and suddenly looked confused.

"Balt mined and crafted this very ring," I whispered as I slid the ring onto her finger.

Loher's eyes lit up with mutual pride as she realized that this ring was extra special.

The King then turned to Loher.

"Loher," the King softly stated, "as you present Thunor with his wedding ring, and pledge your love and life to him, will you please repeat after me:

"Thunor, I give you this ring as a symbol of my love...

With all that I am and all that I have...

I promise to love and honor you, always.

With this ring, I thee wed."

"I'm afraid there's nothing special about this ring," Loher winked as she slid the ring onto my finger.

"Yes there is," I playfully argued, "your heart picked it out."

Loher simply smiled and we turned to face the King.

"And now," the King announced, "with the power vested in me by my father, the King before me and Onh, above all else, I pronounce you, Man and Wife.

Just wait until I'm over there before you kiss," the King pled, "I don't wanna see the mushy stuff."

A collective chuckle arose from the audience.

I swear that The Scorpion herself was applauding as we shared our first marital kiss.

Brother Fost and the Sailors began to play a jaunty sea shanty and the crowd began to move.

Meeka and Kuchoff began casting fireballs and energy balls into the sky above The Scorpion, creating a sort of fireworks show.

"Where be t'e ale?" Balt shouted and began to laugh.

"Balt!" Loher called to the dwarf, "This is the most beautiful ring I've ever seen."

Balt blushed.

"And I'm not just saying that because you made it," Loher qualified.

"Wear it wit' pride," Balt sniffed and turned away, "t'ere's sumptin in me eye again."

Loher and I laughed and began to mix and mingle with our friends.

EPILOGUE

“That was such a moving ceremony,” Meeka sniffed and hugged Loher.

“Thank you,” I beamed, “I especially liked the light show at the end.”

“Kuchoff and I had it planned for a few days,” Meeka giggled.

“Light show?” Loher asked, “I thought that was part of the kiss!”

Meeka and I laughed and tapped the rims of our mugs to Loher's drink.

The night sky was as clear as glass, teaming with billions and billions of stars.

The moon was almost full, or perhaps it was waning, I couldn't be sure.

We were moving at a slower pace than normal, enjoying the warm summer breeze on our skin and blowing through our hair.

A party was in full swing, complete with Kuchoff playing a lute and singing, trying his best to keep a tune.

Loher and I decided to sneak off alone for a while.

Before we could successfully sneak away, Balt caught us, “We're gonna go lookin' fer t'em escaped wizards tamarrow, right?”

“It's going to be difficult,” Loher stated, “but, yes.”

"Guid," Balt smiled, gazed at Loher's new ring for a moment, raised his mug of ale in our direction, "Mister an' Missus McLaaud," he slurred, and then half stumbled away, looking for Rion.

———◆———

We finally found ourselves in the crow's nest, high above the rest of our companions.

The sea was so calm, we could barely feel the sway from the waves.

We could still hear Kuchoff performing, keeping our found family entertained.

People were singing along and laughing.

I could even hear Balt, slightly inebriated, trying to explain a fighting style to Rion, but the dwarf's accent gets thicker the drunker he gets and it was becoming increasingly difficult for the shy eline warrior to understand.

We stood up there in the crow's nest, holding each other, enjoying the peace and calmness in silence.

"So, what was your favorite part?" Loher asked after a while, with closed eyes as she smiled and felt the warm breeze drift around her.

"The moment you said, 'I do.'" I whispered into her ear.

Her smile widened and she gently let her head rest on my shoulder.

"Mine was when Nitch started snoring," she admitted in a giggle, her hand failing to hide it, "his timing was perfect."

I pulled her a little closer and held her a bit tighter as The Scorpion rounded a bend around a small island.

I noticed that the music had suddenly stopped playing and Meeka was frantically asking Kuchoff what was wrong.

Kuchoff didn't respond, he just sat there, lute in hand, but motionless.

The laughter and chatter of conversation slowed and stopped.

"We need to investigate," Loher stated and grabbed my hand.

The climb down from the crow's nest seemed like it took ages, even with gravity on our side.

By the time we arrived on the deck, Kuchoff had gotten up and moved to the side of the ship, peering out into the darkness.

A crowd began to gather near.

"Kuchoff, sweetheart," Meeka pled, "what's wrong? What's going on?

No answer.

He just stood there, as if he was waiting, looking for something.

"Oi!" Balt prodded as he gently nudged Kuchoff with his finger, "Boy-o, are ye okay?"

Nothing.

"Are ya seasick or sumptin'?" Balt asked, trying to get even a small reaction out of his friend.

No reaction.

Not even a blink.

Balt looked at Meeka and sadly shook his head as he gave the teenager some room.

"Should we just leave him alone?" A concerned sailor asked.

"I don't know," Meeka admitted, not breaking her gaze.

"I'll keep an eye on him, Ma'am," the sailor offered.

"That's generous of you," Meeka tried to smile, "I would appreciate the extra eyes."

"I'll be right back," the sailor announced, "I'll go get more men to help keep an eye on him."

"Thank you," Meeka sighed and returned her focus on Kuchoff.

The sailor ran off, calling out to his friends.

"I'm sure everything will be fine soon," Brother Fost commented, trying to keep Meeka calm.

Meeka smiled weakly, "I really hope you're right, Brother Fost," she sighed and leaned against the ship's railing.

Light conversations and a little bit of hushed laughter began as people began to enjoy the festivities once again.

A trio of sailors struck up another old sea shanty and some of our shipmates began to dance.

Moments went by as the sailors and Meeka tried to revive Kuchoff's attention, but all he would do was stand there and stare out to the pitch-dark sea.

Watching.

Waiting?

For what?

For who?

Unexpectantly, Roash let out a sudden hiss and extended her natural claws.

We all began to frantically look around for some sort of danger.

As if from out of nowhere, a dark ship, comparable in size to The Scorpion, appeared from the darkness.

"I leaned closer to Loher, "Talk about perfect timing."

She wasn't very amused.

Dark figures could barely be seen standing at her bow; I counted four.

As the ship grew closer, Kuchoff began to climb up the railing.

Meeka tried to stop him but found herself paralyzed.

Unable to move, Meeka called out, "Kuchoff!"

At that exact moment, the entirety of the approaching ship, now only meters away, suddenly lit up with fiery torchlight, revealing double rows of large cannons, hundreds upon hundreds of well-armed and armored human warriors, orcs, hobgoblins and ogres, as well as the identities of the four figures up front.

Three of them were the escaped wizards we had once captured in the other realm...

"Well," Balt belched, "t'is makes it a whole lot easier ta find 'em."

The fourth figure standing on the bow with the three escapees was a little more difficult to see...

Kuchoff stepped down from the railing, fighting to move, he slowly began to make his way back away from the railing, a horrified look, dripping from his face, when a female voice softly called out from the opposing ship, "Kuuuuchooooff..."

The frightened teenager seemed to gain a little bit more control as he drew his katana and fearfully cried out in terror, "MOM??"

<The End>

If you enjoyed *Vast* please post a review
and watch for Book Four of The Scorpion Chronicles.

Coming soon...